Sweet-Talking TJ

"STELLLAAAA! Don' stop!" Jake roared, wondering why we weren't going anywhere any more.

Ignoring my little brother's demand, I tried yelling again.

"TJ!"

Nothing. If anything, he dropped his head even lower to the ground.

I gripped tightly on to the buggy handle, stunned, as TJ and his mates (and Bob) turned into the alley where The Vault was. One of the lads – couldn't tell 'em apart yet – turned and gave me a sarky little wave before they disappeared.

I still didn't move, though I could feel my cheeks flooding pink. I had just been blanked, by my supposed friend. What in Bob's name was all *that* about?

Also by Karen McCombie:

The *Ally's World* series
Frankie, Peaches & Me

And coming soon:

Meet the Real World, Rachel
Truly, Madly Megan
Amber and the Hot Pepper Jelly

Find out more about Stella Etc. at
www.karenmccombie.com

STELLA. ETC.

SWEET-TALKING TJ

KAREN McCOMBIE

SCHOLASTIC

For Alison, who was Alyx (silent "x") back when we were 14

Scholastic Children's Books,
Commonwealth House, 1–19 New Oxford Street,
London, WC1A 1NU, UK
A division of Scholastic Ltd
London ~ New York ~ Toronto ~ Sydney ~ Auckland
Mexico City ~ New Delhi ~ Hong Kong

First published in the UK by Scholastic Ltd, 2004

Copyright © Karen McCombie, 2004
Cover illustration copyright © Spike Gerrell, 2004

ISBN 0 439 97346 5

Printed and bound by Nørhaven Paperback A/S, Denmark

10 9 8 7 6 5 4 3

CONTENTS

From: *stella*
To: FFFrankie
Subject: Hope you're bored 'cause here's more stufff to read!
Attachments: "Sweet-Talking TJ"

Hi FFFrankie!

Wow . . . Lauren just e-mailed THE most boring e-mail I have ever had in my lifffe. I really miss you lot in London and love hearing fffrom you, but did Lauren *really* need to tell me the shape she fffiled her nails into? I wrote back and told her that ifff she was really fffed up, she should ask her mum and dad ifff she could come and visit me, and we could just have fffun, hanging out at the beach fffeeding fffairy cakes to the psycho seagull and stufff. She hasn't got back to me yet – d'you think I scared her offf by mentioning the psycho seagull?!

Talking about e-mails, in the last one you sent, I couldn't fffigure out what you were on about in your PS – the bit about "who was the boy that answered your mobile?". It did my head in fffor ages, and then it suddenly hit me, and I realized. . .

Hey, you know something? I'm not going to

tell you here, 'cause that'll spoil the surprise. I thought it'd be better ifff I wrote the whole thing down, starting fffrom the night after you got the train back to London, 'cause that's when . . . oops! Nearly blew it again!

Look, just read the attachment and it'll all make sense. (Er. . .)
Miss you ☹, but M8s 4eva ☺!

stella

PS It took me ages to input this because Peaches is sprawled out and snoring *right* in fffront of the keyboard. I have to hit the "FFF" key really hard 'cause of a wodge of ginger fffur stuck under there. . .

CHAPTER 1

Fuzzy eyeballs

Y'know . . . when you cross your eyes, things look really different. (Including you; it makes you look like a right idiot.)

At this moment, my idiotically crossed eyes were gawping across the jumble of tiled rooftops outside my bedroom window, vaguely focusing on the faraway fairground down by the beach. When I squeezed my fuzzy eyeballs together, all the jewel-coloured bulbs on the Big Wheel looked blurrily beautiful, like gently pulsating lights on some alien spacecraft, hovering in the sunset over Portbay. . .

Hey, that was pretty poetic.

Or maybe it just sounds like the rantings of a nutter; I don't know.

Blame my sudden genius/nutter rantings on the fact that it was nine-ish on Sunday night and I was *completely* pour-me-into-bed tired after the weekend. It had all been a bit like the roller

3

coaster me and Frankie had whizzed around on last night, hanging on for dear life and not knowing whether to shriek in total fear or burst into a bad case of the giggles.

So how'd you describe the weekend I'd just had?

Put it this way, if I saw the words "GREAT", "TERRIBLE", "EVEN *MORE* TERRIBLE", "EMOTIONAL", "FUN", and "ZONKED" on a form with tick boxes, I'd tick *every* single one.

I'd tick "GREAT", 'cause Frankie had come to visit me here at the new house (and new town).

I'd tick "TERRIBLE", 'cause she'd acted weird, making me homesick for London, homesick for Seb (the boyfriend I *might* have had), homesick for all my old friends, and homesick for the best, most brilliant mate that Frankie (usually) was.

I'd tick "EVEN *MORE* TERRIBLE", 'cause of Frankie admitting last night that she was the girlfriend Seb definitely *did* have (urgh). And the fact that she admitted it while we were marooned at the top of a broken-down Big Wheel ride didn't exactly help (but that's another story).

I'd tick "EMOTIONAL", 'cause of Frankie and me falling out, then making up again, promising to be friends for ever, and never to let boys and long distances get in the way.

I'd tick "FUN", 'cause of this afternoon's house-warming party – having Auntie V here, as well as Frankie, was ace. And then, through our new neighbour, I got to find out lots of info on the mysterious person who used to live in our house.

And finally, I'd tick "ZONKED", 'cause of all the post-party tidying that had to be done, *and* 'cause of all of the above added together. . .

"Hey, Stella – that was your Aunt Vanessa on the phone!" I heard Dad call up from downstairs. "She's just got back home, but she told me to let you know that she and Frankie managed to get a seat together on the train back to London!"

Actually, I'd just e-mailed Frankie about twenty minutes ago, asking how the trip home had gone (probably had a million spelling mistakes in it I was so tired). I was glad to hear it went OK – even if I wasn't hearing it from *her*.

"Great!" I called out in reply.

I could make out Mum shushing Dad from somewhere, annoyed with him for risking waking the twins. Ha! If they were half as tired as I was, you could yell the theme tune of *EastEnders* through a megaphone at them and they wouldn't move a muscle.

I should've given in and headed for my bed and early snoozeland too, but I didn't have the energy to get up from my kneeling (OK, *slouching*) position on the floor of my room. So I just let my elbows slither further apart on the windowsill and stared – kind of contentedly – into space.

That was until my hazy view of the twinkling Big Wheel was suddenly obscured by a huge black shadow. . .

OK, OK, so it was more of a huge, *ginger* shadow. A ginger shadow that looked fuzzy even once I'd uncrossed my eyes.

"Hi, Peaches!" I smiled at the huge scruffy cat that had silently hopped up on the windowsill and settled its purring self *right* in front of my face.

"Prrrrp!"

I couldn't be absolutely sure what "prrrrp!" meant, but I had a funny feeling that it translated as "I've been curled up in your den in the garden, hiding away from your demented little brothers".

I couldn't blame Peaches if he *had* hidden away; at this afternoon's house-warming party, the twins had somehow managed to eat a whole trifle between them when no one was looking, and spent the next hour roaring around on a sugar high, causing mayhem and resisting all attempts to be caught and have the cream and coloured sugar sprinkles washed off their faces/hands/hair/clothes.

6

"Hey, I saved you some leftover hot dog," I told my cool cat, taking my elbows off the sill to make more room for His Tubbiness. "It's in your bowl in the kitchen. I even washed off the mustard so you don't burn your tongue!"

Peaches' green eyes stared deep into mine, as if he was slowly devouring that edible piece of information. Then he stretched forward, catty nostrils working overtime, until he gently touched his inquisitive nose on to mine, making my eyes go crossed all over again.

By the time I blinked my eyes into focus, he was gone, bounding out of the open window, landing on the kitchen roof with a powder-soft *doofff*, and then padding and pouncing off somewhere wherever. And there I was, left lounging on my bedroom floor, wondering what exactly I smelled of (leftover hot dog?) and if I'd just been given the feline version of a nose-rubbing Eskimo kiss.

"Except the *proper* name for Eskimos is Inuits," I murmured to myself, some module we'd done in geography about societies around the world popping pointlessly into my mushy brain. Of course, I'd learned that at my *old* school, back in London. After the holidays, I'd have a new school, a new geography teacher, and new classmates (gulp). Only five weeks to go (double gulp). . .

To take my mind off that distressing thought, I grabbed a hunk of my T-shirt and sniffed hard, trying to suss out what exactly had got up Peaches' nose just now. Aha – it seemed that today's party and the tidying-up afterwards had left me with barbecue-scented hair and a general waft of Fairy Liquid. Nice. . . .

Bleep!

It was only a tiny, high-pitched noise, but the sound of that incoming text message acted like a big, flashing, neon "GO!!" to my nervous system and I practically *scrambled* over to my bed, grabbing the flashing phone that I'd tossed on there earlier.

Remember – every day! was all it said, but it made me smile. It was from Frankie, that was for sure, reminding me of the promise we'd made to each other on the platform of Portbay station, earlier this evening. From now on, we'd keep in touch – by text, e-mail, letter, phone, jokey postcard or carrier pigeon – every single day, so that the distance between us didn't matter.

"M8s 4eva!" I keyed back to her, thinking how strange it was that she was back in London, and how strange it was that I didn't ache to be there

too, considering how bad I felt about being dragged to this bizarre-o little town only a few days or so ago. But then, so much had changed in such a tiny amount of time: last Sunday, I'd been so miserable about moving to Portbay that it felt like someone had cut out my heart and stuffed a sack of sludge in its place. Then all the weird and kind of wonderful stuff started happening: Peaches moving in, like he'd always lived here; meeting the mad old lady (Mrs Sticky Toffee) with her even madder "pet" (a bad-tempered seagull with a sweet tooth); discovering Sugar Bay, and the secrets of the old, not-so-grand house there.

Amazingly, tonight, instead of yearning for my old life in Kentish Town, I was yearning for tomorrow to come, just to see what other secrets and surprises Portbay had in store for me. . .

Well, my newly reactivated brain might have been mostly full of vibey thoughts, but a tiny part of it was alerting me to an odd noise coming from somewhere outside.

"Bark!" [thump] "Bark!" [thump] "Bark!"

Dropping the phone back down on the duvet, I got up and wandered over to the open window.

"Bark!" [thump] "Bark!" [thump] "Bark!"

At the end of our overgrown tangle of a back

garden, just over the tall brick wall that you can hardly see for tangle, there's a tiny lane that ambles between all the mismatching houses and cottages in our corner of the town. Right now, just above the top of the wall, I could make out a furry brown head – which appeared with a bark, before disappearing with a thump.

What's that dumb dog up to? I wondered to myself, watching its Jack-in-the-box routine.

And then I got it: Peaches.

In the couple of minutes since he'd flounced off the windowsill and left me to my mobile messaging, Peaches had perched himself comfortably on the garden wall, all the better to peer at passers-by – human and canine – on this warm, summer's evening. And now he was being peered at himself, by an over-enthusiastic four-legged "friend".

For a second there, I panicked, feeling a protective flurry of worry for Peaches, but then I realized I was wasting my time. I mean, I guess that any *normal* cat – faced with barking and big teeth at close quarters – would now be off like a shot, hissing and spitting, doing the whole arched-back thing. But not my Peaches. He was calmly squatting, paws tucked under his ample belly, watching this frantic, manic dog with nothing more than mild interest, the way you might let your eyes settle on a meandering dust-speck if you were spectacularly bored.

"Bob! C'mere! Leave the puss alone!" I heard a boy's voice suddenly urge.

I was glad to hear that someone was in charge of the mental mutt, but it couldn't have been a very grown-up or tall someone – I couldn't see a hint of anyone above the adult-sized wall.

"Bark!" [thump] "Bark!" [thump] "Bark!"

"Bob! I said *down*, boy!"

Whoever the kid was and however young he was, the dog thankfully did what he was told and gave up with a gruff "Awww, spoilsport!" grumble.

"You idiot! Don't you remember the *last* time you tried to lick a cat?" I heard a voice chatter, as the kid and "Bob" set off down the lane. "It took *months* for your nose to heal. . ."

As the voice, the dog-panting, footsteps and claw-taps faded away along the cobblestoned lane, I gazed down at Peaches, who at that exact same second turned and looked up at me. And *winked*.

Wow, that cat sure was weird. . .

CHAPTER 2

Bob, the boy and the dive-bombing bird

Well, shock, horror: Jake and Jamie were playing nicely.

OAPs strolling past us on the beach cooed at the boys, who were happily digging and patting at their sandcastle, chubby hands clutched around plastic buckets and spades.

"Aren't they adorable!" said one older lady, stopping to smile down at the general cuteness.

"Like little angels!" said her friend, tilting her white-haired head.

"Mmmm!" I mumbled in reply, shading the sun from my eyes with my hand as I smiled up at the two elderly ladies who were obviously besotted with my brothers. Ha! They wouldn't have called Jake and Jamie angels if they had seen them this morning, having joint toddler tantrums and then a kicking competition, all over a quarrel about a piece of jammy toast.

("Er, Louise. . ." my dad had grinned at my

mum, as they each grabbed a twin before the boys put any serious dents into each other, "can you just remind me – *why* did we decide to have more kids after Stella?")

"Are they brothers, or just little friends?"

"Brothers. *My* brothers," I replied, not surprised at the woman's question, since the twins weren't identical, and none of the three of us looked particularly alike. "They're twins, actually."

"Twins? Oh, how lovely!" said her friend. "Twice the fun!"

("Do you think it's too late to take them back to the shop and get a refund?" my mum had joked drily to my dad, hoisting a wriggling, ranting Jake in the air earlier.)

"So boys, what are your names, hmm?" the first lady asked, bending over and ruffling the nearest two-year-old head, which happened to be Jamie's. My heart was suddenly in my mouth: my mate Eleni back in London has this sweet little Jack Russell called Dixie that no one can resist petting when her family takes him for a walk. Then Eleni or whoever always has to launch into this big apologizing thing after Dixie has nipped a chunk out of the well-meaning stranger's hand. The trouble is, Jamie isn't as fussy as Dixie; stranger, sister, friend, foe, fellow toddler, OAP . . .

he'll bite anyone if he's in the mood. I held my breath and silently prayed that he *wasn't* in the mood.

"NEMO!" yelled Jamie, grinning widely enough to show off his fine rows of baby teeth. (Good: *showing* was cool; *using* wasn't.)

"GONZO!" yelled Jake, throwing his head back for full roaring effect.

"Oh, um . . . those are *very* unusual names!" muttered the lady who'd asked the question. In that split second, I could practically read her thoughts: "I don't know; parents these days! Why can't they give their children *sensible* names?" But before I could explain that Jamie was obsessed with his new bucket and spade set (decorated with scenes from Disney's *Finding Nemo*), and that Jake was just yelling out the nickname my Auntie V has for him (after a character from the old Muppets TV show), a sudden honk distracted her.

"Maureen – I think that's our bus driver tooting. We'd better get a move on!" said Maureen's friend, nodding at the day-trippers' coach up on the prom.

"Yes, we better had. Well, bye, dear! Bye, er, boys!"

The three of us – me, Nemo and Gonzo – waved at the departing ladies, as they struggled to hurry across the hot golden sands that seemed to swallow up their sandals with every step.

"Big ladies go wibble-wobble," Jamie/Nemo announced, loudly enough for a bunch of nearby bikini'd sunbathers to start sniggering.

Yikes.

When I saw the four girls push themselves up on their elbows and look over at us, I felt myself blushing, and quickly rummaged around in the sand for my half-buried sunglasses to hide behind. It wasn't *just* the fact that my brothers were embarrassment on four legs, it was more the fact that I recognized those girls: they were the same crew that did a stare-a-thon on me that first time I went into the Shingles café with Mum and the boys. And let's just say that from their sneers, they sure let me know *exactly* what they thought of me. (Clue: not much.)

"Er, whatever . . . and little boys go dig, dig, right?" I said, turning and trying to restart the twins' interest in their sandcastle, before they embarrassed me any more.

Luckily, digging *did* seem more interesting than shouting after wibbly-wobbly big ladies, and the boys went back to creating what looked like Camelot to *them*, and a big mound of sand to everyone else. And luckily, the girls from the café slid back down on to their towels and carried on burning themselves pink.

Which gave me the chance to pull out my mobile and talk to a friendly face, even if I couldn't see it.

"Frankie? S'me!" I smiled, turning my head away from the direction of the café crew so they didn't get a chance to earwig on my conversation.

"Hey, Stella! I was just going to e-mail you!"

"Yeah? What were you going to say?"

"Just thanks for the e-mail you sent last night – I picked it up this morning. And just to tell you that I ended up sitting with your Auntie V all the way back on the train last night."

"Too late – I knew that already. Dad spoke to Auntie V last night!" I told her, ruffling grains of sand through the fingers of one hand and idly people-watching from behind the safety of my sunglasses at the same time. (Facing this way, I could see a family racing each other squealing into the sea; the blokes up in the prom car park dismantling the fairground rides; a bored-looking indie kid boy kicking along the sand with a hairy dog and a singing, skipping little girl in tow.)

"Yeah? Well, that's saved valuable writing time, I guess! So what're you up to, Stell?"

"I'm at the beach, babysitting the boys."

"Why? What are your mum and dad doing?"

"Dad's heavily into his DIY today—"

"He's wrecking the house some more, you mean?" Frankie said cheekily (and truthfully).

"Yep. And Mum's at the hairdresser."

I was hoping that Mum wouldn't be too long; it wasn't that I was stressing out about looking after the boys or anything, it was just that I was itching to get to Woolworths and check out their photo frames, dull as that might sound to anyone else. But it wasn't dull to me; I'd promised myself that I'd get a nice frame for the black and white snapshot Mum had come across at the weekend. For the moment, it was pinned to a corkboard in my den in the garden (i.e. the outhouse Dad had helped me clear out). But it was too precious to leave like that; because a) it was the one and only photo I had of Nana Jones and Grandad Eddie together, and b) it was the one and only photo of people in my family who looked *anything* like me.

Y'see, I hadn't inherited my dad's tall, blond looks, and I didn't look much like my mum, with her olive skin and long, dark, straight hair. (At least, I *hoped* it was still long, dark and straight when the hairdresser had finished with her.) But anyway, I'd gone a bit shivery on Saturday night, when Mum shoved the photo under my freckly nose, 'cause *there* was my pretty Nana Jones (aged seventeen), with a mass of freckles sprinkled over her *own* pale nose, and there was her boyfriend (Grandad Eddie, aged eighteen), a handsome young black guy with his hair like a dark halo against the brightly painted backdrop of the fairground where he worked.

It was just a pity that I couldn't meet them in person, to talk about how much of a pain freckles are with my Nana Jones, and ask Grandad Eddie if he liked my golden-brown version of his own dark afro curls. But neither of them was around, mainly 'cause one of them died years ago (Nana Jones) and one of them had vanished (Grandad Eddie, about six weeks after the photo had been taken and *before* Nana Jones could tell him that she was expecting my mum).

Still, you can't change what you can't change, as Frankie's mum used to say; and she's very fond of her sayings, is Frankie's mum. I was just thrilled that my mum had come across the photo at all, and that I had this tiny but important piece of my own history. . .

"Bob! *No!*"

"Who's that?" Frankie asked, her natural nosiness picking up on the boyish, shouting voice close by me.

"Er . . . I dunno," I said, hardly able to talk about someone who was only standing about a metre away. And then I heard a boy in the background at Frankie's end too.

"Hey, Stella – Mum's just let Seb in. Look, can I call you back later?"

"Sure, talk to you later," I nodded to no one in particular, wondering how long it would be before Frankie stopped feeling awkward about mentioning Seb, since (amazingly) it didn't really bother me much any more.

"*Bob!* What did I *say*?"

Pressing the end-call button on the phone, I immediately zoned in on the look of alarm on both my brothers' faces as a *very* large, *very* hairy Alsatian loomed over them, lifted his leg and prepared to pee over Camelot.

"Down, *now*!"

"Hurfff?" gruffed the dog, as it lowered its leg and stared up dolefully at the boy hollering at it.

"*Naughty* Bob! *Naughty* Bob! Bob's a very *naughty* dog!" a blonde little girl sing-songed to the Alsatian, who turned its hairy head and gazed at her with mild confusion.

(Uh-oh – all the commotion had got the café crew up on their elbows for a nosey, I couldn't help but notice out of the corner of my eye.)

"C'mere!" the boy ordered, trying to sound stern and pointing to his side. I wasn't sure if he was talking to the pooch or the little girl (his sister?), but as the girl took no notice of him and kept skipping barefoot, daisy-decorated sandals swinging in her hand, I guessed it was the pooch.

Like a kid who's just been told off, "Naughty Bob" reluctantly ambled where he was told, by the boy's side, his head held sulkily low. Meanwhile, the little girl started skipping around the sandcastle, merrily singing her "Naughty Bob" song, while the twins stared at her with the same mildly confused expressions the dog had on its fuzzy face just now.

"Sorry," the boy said, with a cute grin a mile wide. "Thought you were about to get a moat around your castle then!"

Pretty funny.

"I guess!" I laughed, scrambling to my feet to talk to him (and keeping my back to the café crew so they couldn't put me off). "He's cute!"

As I patted the hairy bundle of dog, I was chuffed to notice that there was no sign of my first-time-speaking-to-someone stammer. Though to be honest, *that* only tended to rear its head when I was nervous – in front of anyone remotely older than me, or especially when it came to people around my own age. But now that I was standing up next to this lad, er, make that *towering over* him, I sussed out that he could have only been about ten, or maybe eleven, which made my lack of stammering make sense, if you see what I mean.

"Yeah, he's great, but he's just a bit thick!" the boy continued, rubbing the top of the dog's head so hard it shook, which earned him a tongue-lolling smile from "Bob".

Bob . . . of course.

"Y'know, I *saw* you last night. Or at least a bit of your dog," I said, rewinding Bob's Jack-in-the-box trick in my head. "He was barking at my cat in the alleyway behind my house!"

The boy frowned for a second, pushing the floppy fair hair back off his face as he tried to figure out what I was on about. It didn't take too long.

"Ah, right! That cat – what's its name again? Peaches! He's living with you now, is he?"

"Uh-huh," I said nodding, remembering what Mrs Sticky Toffee had said about Peaches' wandering spirit. It still seemed funny to think that people around the town knew Peaches already, when I was just starting to feel like he belonged to me. Or more like *I* belonged to him. . .

"So you've moved in to that old dump in Dingle Lane?" the boy asked bluntly, the smile freezing on his face when he realized what he'd said.

"Don't worry," I told him, smiling so he knew I wasn't horribly offended. "It *is* a bit of a dump! But my dad's doing it up, so it should be pretty nice . . . by the time I'm thirty-five, maybe!"

Hey, I made a joke! And I got a laugh! Back home in London with my old gang, it was always Frankie or Neisha or one of the other girls that made the jokes and got the laughs, never shy old *me*.

"Yeah – that place could be OK," said the boy, trying to sound positive and undo the boo-boo he'd made. "I, uh, probably should just keep my mouth shut, but I sneaked in there once, when it was empty. There was a broken window. Had a nosey around and everything!"

That was a bit weird to hear too. I mean, our house had sat unloved and unlived-in for *years* before my mum and dad bought it, but it was funny (peculiar, not ha-ha) to think that this lad might have wandered around my room before I'd ever set eyes on its peeling walls.

Still, what did it matter? Hadn't I gone noseying around the old, deserted, dilapidated mansion in Sugar Bay, once or twice – OK, make that *three* times – this last week? What *did* matter was that this was the first conversation I was having with someone even *vaguely* near my own age since I'd moved here, and I didn't want it to stop. I was just about to try another joke – something pathetic like asking him if he'd needed to call Jungle Rescue to find his way out of our hugely overgrown garden – when a funny (peculiar) thing happened.

"Don't move. Please!"

The boy hurriedly stepped directly in front of me, and was hunkering his head down into his shoulders, like he was trying to do a turtle impersonation and make his head disappear into his scruffy, khaki, army-style shirt. Confused, I cast my eyes right (nothing, apart from vaguely curious café crew, who were whispering amongst themselves), and then left (and just saw my brothers, who were now skipping Pied Piper-style behind the little girl, followed by Bob, who was sniffing madly at what looked suspiciously like a bit of jammy toast peeking out of Jake's pocket).

"What is it? What's wrong?" I asked, feeling suddenly like a human shield.

"It's just some lads I know. Er, mates, I s'pose. Just don't want to see them right now."

I couldn't figure out *why* you might not want

23

to see your so-called mates, but what I *could* figure out was that they must be somewhere directly behind me. With a quick swivel of my head, I turned and spotted four guys, slouching grouchily along the prom.

"*They're* your *mates*?"

I turned back to face the cowering boy whose name I didn't know yet and frowned. OK, so I didn't know a *lot* of stuff about him, but it didn't seem, well, *right* somehow that those slouchy, grouchy lads could be people he'd hang out with. For a start, they were a lot older than him (they were at least fifteen, I reckoned), and second, they looked like *trouble*. (Actually, what they also looked like was familiar, weirdly enough. . .)

"Yeah, well . . . kind of. It's just— Oh, God, not *now*!"

I heard the flap of wings a millisecond before the ear-splitting cawing started up.

"Gerraway! *Gerroff!*" the boy yelped, stumbling about and doing plenty of flapping himself, as a huge seagull began dive-bombing him.

"Shoo!" I said feebly, then stopped as a flash of recognition hit me. Was it the same one I kept seeing? The one with the sweet tooth (sweet beak?) that Mrs Sticky Toffee fed fairy cakes to?

Maybe I should do a Bob and grab that jammy

piece of toast off Jake and see if I can lure it away, I thought frantically, wondering what exactly this big bird had against this potential new friend of mine.

Speaking of Bob. . .

"Bark! Bark! Bark!" Bob woofed madly, leaving the Pied Piper trail and coming to the rescue of his master.

And then I heard *another* noise above the shouting, cawing, barking commotion: cackling.

At first I suspected the café crew – who, sure enough, were sniggering themselves stupid again – but the source of the cackle was *way* too deep and blokey for them. I turned and saw the gang of lads, now leaning on the blue prom railings, presumably to stop themselves from falling down laughing at the sight of their mate's predicament.

"Hey, Deejay!" one of them yelled over. "Got to watch out for that seagull, mate! The size of you, it could lift you up and carry you away!"

The rest of the lads went into cackling overdrive at that dig – and *that's* when I knew where I recognized them from. They were the boys who'd laughed at me in the Shingles café last weekend, when I ended up with Jake's tomato sauce handprints on the front of my T-shirt. *And*

they were the same ones Frankie had blown a cheeky kiss at and made a fool of when she was here. . .

Anyway, never mind me: the cackling definitely got a reaction from the boy. He flushed through eight shades of pink as he glanced at the lads, then at the café crew, then at me.

"Ellie, come on – let's go!" he suddenly ordered his skipping, singing maybe-sister, while the seagull circled higher, out of Bob's barking way.

"'Deejay. . .?" I muttered to myself, my eyes fixed on the boy's speedily retreating back, as he scarpered along the sands, head down and cheeks vivid. Behind him, his maybe-sister and his dog skipped and galloped. Above them all, the seagull swirled ominously.

What would that day-tripping old lady make of someone landing their kid with a name like "Deejay" – specially if she thought Nemo and Gonzo were bad? I couldn't help wondering.

"Bye, doggie!" Jake called after them in a disappointed voice.

"Bye, girl!" Jamie called out, ditto.

My brothers looked like they hadn't a clue what had just gone on. Well, I might have been eleven years older than them, but I didn't have much of a clue either. What in Bob's name was all that hiding, teasing and dive-bombing all about?

Hey, it looked like it was just another weird day in bizarre-o Portbay. . .

ChAPTeR 3

A lot of naff, with a touch of twee

I'd been worried that Mum would go into the hairdresser's with a semi-decent, semi-grown-out haircut, and come out looking like she was wearing a bad wig for a joke.

The reason I didn't hold out much hope for her getting anything remotely resembling a half-decent haircut was that the woman who ran the place had hairsprayed blonde candyfloss perched on her head, which was strangely similar to the doggy hairdos of the two pet shih-tzus flopped on the salon floor. Also, the fact that the owner seemed oblivious to the spelling mistake on her shop sign didn't make me trust her judgement too much either.

But now I took it all back: the Style Compony had actually done a pretty good job.

"Quite nice, isn't it?" Mum asked, glimpsing the reflection of her long, layered, dark bob in the window that we and the buggy were parked in front of.

"Yeah, it is nice," I nodded, taking a lick of the ice-cream cone she'd just bought me. "But I'm still planning on sneaking down here one night with a ladder and some paint and putting that sign right!"

"What, doing some spelling graffiti, you mean?" said Mum, grinning at me over the top of her lemon sorbet.

It was fun just hanging out with her, talking rubbish, mooching around the few shops that Portbay had to offer. The thing about Mum is, she's great (and really groovy, according to all my friends), but hanging-out time together – just me and her – was always pretty limited. *Pre*-twins, it was 'cause she worked long hours in the marketing department of the same magazine compony (sorry, *company* – it's catching!) that Dad used to work for. And then *post*-twins . . . well, one sweet-natured little baby would have kept her busy enough, I guess, but *two* boisterous babies meant there were times when I didn't really get a look-in. Still, to make up for dragging me away from London, Mum seemed to be making a big effort. Or maybe she was just a bit more relaxed here in Portbay. And it sure helped right now that both the boys were sound asleep and drooling in their double buggy, after a hard morning's work creating their mega sand mound (without moat).

"Anyway, you still haven't chosen your favourite," Mum reminded me, nodding at the display inside the window, which we'd been gawping at before her reflection caught our attention.

The shop we'd stopped at was the Portbay Galleria, although it should really have been called the Portbay Nafferia, since every piece of locally made art and craftiness lovingly exhibited could have won top prizes in a national Naff competition, with consolation prizes in the "Twee" and "Rotten" categories. There were dozens of seashorey landscapes, all duller than the last one. There were clay figurines of jolly fishermen, jolly smugglers, and jolly pirates, who all looked like the same jolly guy; with the sculptor swapping a sword for a swag-bag, or an eyepatch for a fish, depending on which character he was trying to capture. (Mum said she hoped he never got muddled and ended up sticking a haddock instead of a parrot on the pirate's shoulder.) There were sets of crystal fish, which consisted of hunks of crystal with googly plastic eyes and the odd fin stuck on. There were bits of driftwood carved into shells, shells glued together into something that *might* have been a frolicking seal (or haddock), and even bog-standard stones with the word "Portbay" painted on them, specially made for those tourists suffering from a severe lack of taste.

"I think the lampshade made out of dried seaweed is my favourite," I decided finally. "Think of the pong once you've had the light on for a while!"

"Yeah, well that *is* bad," Mum agreed, "but the worst one's *got* to be the painting of the mermaid, hasn't it?"

Actually, Mum was right. There were a few paintings by the same artist – of the usual fishermen, pirates and smugglers mostly – but they all had one thing in common; terrible fingers. Since drawing's just about my favourite thing to do, I know how hard hands can be, but if I was as bad as *this* artist, I'd stick to bland landscapes, or make the people in my paintings hide their hands behind useful props, like boats, treasure chests and large parrots. I mean, the muddle at the end of each arm was distracting enough when you studied the fishermen, pirates and smugglers, but it looked particularly awful on the serene mermaid, perched on her rock, scales shining, hair tumbling . . . and a bunch of sausages in her lap.

"Looks like there hasn't been a good local artist in this town since Miss Grainger!" said Mum, talking about the old lady who we'd just found out owned our house, decades ago.

Once upon that faraway time, Elize Grainger had used my den as an art studio, and I had one of her delicate fairy paintings – discovered and dusted off – up on the wall in her honour.

"But never mind Miss Grainger – *your* stuff's miles better than most of this lot, Stella!"

As soon as Mum said that, a faint haze of lime and sugar-pink caught my eye in the glass of the window. Spinning around, I expected to see Mrs Sticky Toffee strolling along the prom, her meringue netting hat keeping the sun off her head, her shiny green raincoat flapping in the breeze, swinging her tiny bag crammed with sweet treats for any human/cat/seagull she happened to come across. Whether the mad old dear knew it or not, she'd got me kind of interested in this town and all its stories, and since I'd got Mum's attention, I'd have loved to point her out.

But there was no one there. Well, no one apart from a whole crowd of holidaymakers, I mean, and the only pink on view was a few lobster-shaded people who'd lain on the beach too long and were too stupid to use sunblock.

Speaking of which. . .

"Hey, look at this," said Mum, pushing the buggy along the pavement and reading a notice that was just being stuck up on the shop door. "Fancy joining the local Knitting and Crochet Society, Stella?"

Mum was only fooling around, but right at that moment I found it hard to smile, since the person Sellotaping the sign on the other side of the glass door was one of the sunbathing café crew from earlier. What was she doing? Did she have a holiday job here or something? It would have to be a pretty laid-back job, if the boss let you have sunbathing breaks with your mates. . .

"I'd rather have a hole drilled in my head," I said, talking about joining the Knitting and Crochet Society, but the same could have been said about the idea of hanging out with this girl and the rest of the café crew. The girl probably thought the same thing about me; the second she clocked me standing outside, she turned her pretty, but pretty *sulky* face and walked away into the depths of the shop.

"Well, what about Dog Training classes?" Mum suggested, pointing to another sign. "You could take Peaches along and say he was a rare breed of Himalayan lion dog!"

"Or I could take Jake and Jamie – it would be handy to teach them to walk on a lead!" I joked back, relaxing now that I wasn't being given the evil eye any more.

"Ah, now *this* actually looks vaguely interesting," said Mum, leaning closer to read yet *another* sign. "Did you know it's the Portbay Gala Week in a fortnight's time?"

"Er, no. . ."

I was only half-listening – my attention had been grabbed again by something reflected in the window.

"There's going to be lots of events taking place all over town. Could be a laugh! Oh, and what's this? *'Tiny Acorns Play Workshop for 2 to 5 year olds'.* That could be fun for the boys, couldn't it?"

"I s'pose. . ."

I'd kind of zoned out of what Mum was saying as I watched a gang of lads stomping along the sands in a laughing scrum. I could've been wrong – since I couldn't see him – but I had a feeling that Deejay was somewhere in the middle of that scrum, mainly 'cause his blonde maybe-sister and Bob the dog were tagging along behind, a safe distance away. That was odd: half an hour ago he couldn't get away from those lads fast enough. . .

Remember that boy's voice you heard in the background today? Well, his name's Deejay, and he's only a kid, really, but we got talking and he was a laugh, I wrote in my head, thinking of the e-mail I'd send Frankie once I got home. *But there's something weird going on with him and these older lads he's hanging out with – think they're the same ones you blew a kiss at in the café when you were here – and I really, really want to know what it's all about. . .*

And then I pressed the "delete" button in my brain and wiped my unwritten message. From the way she'd acted on the phone earlier, it was pretty obvious that Frankie was still hung up on guilt about dating Seb – which made me worry that if I wrote all that stuff then she'd jump on the word "boy" and get all excited at the prospect of me having someone *else* to have a crush on, ignoring the fact that Deejay was a) a stranger, and b) only came up to my *knees*.

No, I wouldn't mention him to Frankie till I knew more, except I wasn't exactly sure *how* I could make that happen. . .

CHAPTER 4

The sound of quiet hammering

Super-cool Peaches was acting like an idiot kitten, skittering around my bedroom floor. Well, I guess Peaches was a bit too tubby to do anything as kitten-like as skittering; I guess you'd probably call it waddling-at-high-speed.

Deejay has to be a nickname, right? I thought to myself, as I stepped out of Peaches' way and grabbed a clean, sand-free T-shirt from my drawer. *His friends must have given it to him, 'cause he's really into music or something...*

Speaking of music, while I got changed and mused over the boy at the beach, I had a CD on, really low, since the twins were still out for the count. (Mum and me had more or less *tipped* them out of their buggy and into their cots for their afternoon nap when we got back home.) The volume wasn't up loud enough to drown out the slow, tinny, tiny *tap-tap-tapping* coming from downstairs though. Ever heard of someone hammering quietly? Well, I think that's what Dad was trying to do now, as he worked on dismantling our old bathroom. Who knew what *that* was going to look like when he was finished, since DIY and Dad went together like bananas and Bovril. Back in London, he couldn't tell which end of a screwdriver was which, but since we'd moved here, he was determined to reinvent himself as Bob the Builder. I just worried that we'd end up with a shower that pumped out arctic-cold water and a toilet that flushed every time you turned the taps on. . . .

Clunk!

"What've you got there, Peaches?" I asked, bending down with a frown to see what he was batting about between his paws. I wasn't scared it was a mouse or anything with a pulse – living things don't usually tend to go *clunk!*

Peaches stopped, panting slightly, and gazed up at me with his knowing green eyes. Between two fat, furry front paws was a marble; shiny clear glass with a twist of ribboned green through the middle. The *clunk!* had been the sound of the marble hitting my mobile, which must have fallen out of the sandy shorts I'd kicked off a couple of minutes ago, and scooted just out of sight under the bed.

37

"Thanks for finding that," I told Peaches, as if he knew what I was on about. "I'd have been in a panic later, thinking I'd lost it or something!"

Just as I went to straighten up, a gleam from the marble made me stop. It dawned on me that it was the sort of small, shiny, irresistible thing that one of my brothers would spot straight away and shove up any nostril going.

"Sorry – I'd better take this," I said, pinching up the marble. For a second, I held it just in the middle of Peaches' forehead, so that he looked like he had one of those spooky third eyes that you get in old Buddhist or Hindu paintings. (I couldn't remember which – I'd have to ask Parminder next time I spoke to her; *she'd* know. Er, except she's Sikh, I think.) All I *did* know – sort of – was that third eyes were meant to represent spiritual powers, like telepathy or something.

It suits you, I told Peaches in my head, testing his telepathic powers. His Ginger Tubbiness looked up at me with all three eyes, and I *know* it was a trick of the light, but I could have *sworn* he blinked all three. . .

And then the message service on my mobile chose that exact moment to ring, just about startling me out of my skin.

"Hey, Stell! It's me, Lauren!" my friend's recorded voice chirped in my ear. How had I missed her call? Must have been after I chucked off my shorts, when I was in the bathroom washing sand out of my ears. *"Just bumped into Frankie and Seb on the High Street a few minutes ago, and she said she'd been talking to you this morning."*

From somewhere downstairs, there came a sudden loud crash, followed by a reverberating clank, and then a very odd strangulated sort of roar. What *was* Dad up to? I walked over to the door to close it, so I could hear Lauren's message better.

"Did she tell you that I'm definitely going to go through with getting my belly button pierced tomorrow afternoon? Eeeeeeek! I'm excited but scared. You know me and needles!"

Oddly enough, as I got to the door, I realized that the only noises coming from downstairs were Dad's quiet hammering and the clatter of cutlery in the kitchen as Mum sorted out lunch. So where was that clanking, roaring racket coming from?

"So what are you up to right now – you're not hanging out at that dumb, deserted house again, are you? Beware of the ghosts of Elize and Joseph! Hee hee!"

39

Lauren was joking about Joseph's house, the old, dilapidated mansion in Sugar Bay – Frankie must have told her all about it. At the weekend, Frankie'd tried her best to seem interested in all the history mystery stuff I'd found out about the family that used to live there, but I could tell she found it about as exciting as watching nail varnish dry, specially since Lauren was now talking about it like it was an episode of *Scooby Doo*. . .

"*Anyway, I'm really glad everything is cool between you and Frankie after the weekend – we all hated knowing about her and Seb and not being able to tell you. And it's brilliant that you're so cool about it too. Um, you are, aren't you?*"

As I listened to Lauren's byes, I made a mental note to phone her back after lunch and tell her yeah, I really, *really* was OK about Frankie and Seb, hoping that all my *other* mates in London weren't fretting that I was just putting a brave face on. . .

I switched off the phone and walked over to the window. Uh-oh: more clanking, a loud THUD! and then a long, drawn-out *screechhHH* . . . all weird and all coming from the house across the back lane from us, I was now pretty sure.

Which is why ten seconds and a short cut

(learned from Peaches) later, I was lowering myself off the kitchen roof and down the old coal bunker, ready to go investigate further.

"Hey, Miss Mountain-climber!" Mum called out of the back door, having heard me slip out of my bedroom window and pad over the ceiling above her. "Lunch'll be ready in about five minutes, so don't go too far!"

"OK! Just going to check something out!" I said, giving her the thumbs-up, while carefully taking giant steps over the knee-high jumble of wild flowers, regular flowers and nipping nettles. A few well-placed bounds, and I was at the back wall, scouring the ground for old pots or bricks I could stand on.

CLANK!

Drat — who knows what was lurking underneath the undergrowth (rusting cars? Roman ruins? bottomless wells?) but one thing was for sure, there were no useful pots or bricks.

CLANK! CLANK! *ScreeeeeeecchhhHHHH!*

Course, there was always the old chair in the den; I could go and grab that and get a better look over the wall. . .

THUDDY-THUDDY-THUD-THUD, *booooooinnnggg!*

As the noises got more mental all of a sudden, I ditched the idea of getting the chair and just *jumped*, trying to sneak a peek over the wall, over the lane, and into any of the windows of the house opposite. The *first* time, I didn't jump high enough and only got an attractive, close-up view of the moss near the top of the wall. The *second* time, I managed to focus for a millisecond on the upper half of a downstairs window. The *third* time, I thought I saw a vague shape of someone through the glass, and then instantly realized – mid-jump – that if *they* saw *me*, I'd look exactly like Bob the dog had last night.

"Stella, what are you up to?" Mum called out from the open kitchen window.

Poor Mum; she must have thought her one and only daughter had completely flipped, watching me pogoing at the bottom of the garden one minute, and then cracking up at some private joke in my mad little head the next.

It was one of those daft moments that I'd normally have loved to tell Frankie about. And I guess I could still have e-mailed her about it in a little while, but somehow the silliness of it all might not have seemed so funny, with her being so far away. What I could really use was a here-

and-now friend to share dumb, daft moments with.

Deejay. . .

Still standing by the wall, my mind somehow slithered back on to the boy from this morning. Could he possibly be a possible friend? Still, he was a bit young. But then, he wasn't 112 or furry, like Mrs Sticky Toffee or Peaches – the only other locals I'd got to know in Portbay so far.

Speaking of a furry local, Peaches chose that moment to appear from nowhere in particular, and began happily curving himself around my bare legs.

"Maybe you can read my mind, fatso," I muttered, heaving him up into my arms and getting a nose full of ginger fluff, "but I wish you could laugh at my jokes!"

"Ha ha HA!" came a rumbling guffaw that sent the hairs on my neck standing to attention.

Through my fingers, I felt most of the fur on Peaches' back do the same thing. His deep green eyes looked at me; my light-brown eyes stared back at him, and I knew – telepathically or not – that we were thinking the same thing: *Huh?*

"Take that! And THAT!"

Rat-a-tat-TAT! Thumpety-thumpety-*thump*. . .

43

I didn't know about Joseph's house, but I suddenly started to wonder if the cottage over the lane from us was haunted – by the ghosts of psycho sumo wrestlers, by the sound of it. . .

CHAPTER 5

Stalking Deejay

"Well, if someone wants to go clanking and thunking around their own house, it's none of our business, really, is it?" Dad had said yesterday, when we were having our lunch, listening to the clanking and thunking and everything else going on in the background.

"Yes," Mum had agreed, picking a large lump of plaster out of Dad's hair before it fell in his minestrone soup. "Between the boys thundering around and your dad demolish— er, working on our place, we can hardly moan about someone *else's* noise, can we?"

My parents were really, seriously, *annoyingly* un-curious about the goings-on in the house over the lane, but I guess that had something to do with living in London for so long. Every area has its own, unique customs, and in London, people have this habit of pretending that weird stuff is normal, especially on the tube. I mean, you could find yourself sitting opposite someone who's dressed in a deeply loopy way, but the rules are that you must carry on reading your copy of *Mizz* or whatever and act like you come across people wearing wellies, a kilt and Stetson *all* the time. It's the same with neighbours; where I used to live, no one would have dreamt of telling Clive our singing neighbour to get back inside and stop howling ancient Frank Sinatra hits out of his window – no matter *how* much him and Frank were doing people's heads in.

Anyway, all of yesterday afternoon, I hung out in my den in the garden, aiming to do lots of drawing but instead getting distracted by the many mysterious noises coming from next door. "You need binoculars," Lauren had suggested, when I called her back yesterday afternoon. "Then you can spy on your neighbours from your bedroom window!" There were only two problems with Lauren's suggestion: 1) We didn't have binoculars, and 2) I wasn't an expert on legal stuff, but I was pretty sure spying on your neighbours through binoculars was ever so slightly against the law.

Then today, bizarrely enough, there wasn't a clank, *aaaarrrgghhh!*, THUNK! or screech to be heard. Maybe sumo-wrestling poltergeists have Tuesdays off, I don't know. But without strange noises to listen out for, I felt at a loose end, and decided to stuff a pad and my chalk pencils into my backpack and go and find something to draw. (Or maybe find a shop that rented binoculars. . .)

I'd never fancied anyone with a pierced lip, black eyeliner and a Marilyn Manson T-shirt before. But the lad leaning on the counter, chatting on the phone, was seriously cute (in a scary way).

"So I says to *him*, 'You don't want to use Logic Audio 5.5 with OSX 10.2, 'cause it doesn't support VST plug-ins!'"

I hadn't a clue what he was on about, but the longer the scary/gorgeous guy waffled on in strange techno-speak, the longer I got to sneak a peek at him, from above the row of vintage comics I was pretending to rifle through.

He was about seventeen, had spiky black hair (dyed), great cheekbones and a (ouch!) pierced lip. He'd have been the-one-everyone-fancies in a boy band, if grunge/goth lads ever formed themselves into boy bands, and I didn't think they did.

So what was I doing, gawping at a lad who was definitely not my type? Well, it was all Bob the dog's fault, kind of. I'd been scuffing down the High Street, on the way to the beach, when a mournful "Howwww-ooooo!" grabbed my attention. And there was Bob, down an alley I hadn't noticed before, sitting outside a shop, beside a metal board sign that read "The Vault – Rare Grooves and Vintage Comix".

Feeling like it might be my destiny to detour, I ambled up the alley, scratched Bob's head, decided that there was a dyslexic sign writer on the loose in Portbay ("Comix"?), and then took the plunge and wandered inside "The Vault" to see if Bob's owner happened to be in there. Not that I had a clue what to say to him if he was.

Coming in from bright sunshine outside, it had taken my eyes a while to adjust to the gloom in The Vault. The Vault wasn't a vault, by the way (though it looked and smelled like one). It was just your standard shop, but one that could definitely have done with a *Changing Rooms* style transformation. Maybe Laurence Llewelyn-Bowen and the design team could have zoomed around and replaced the black paint on the walls, ceiling and shelving racks for something more vibrant and soothing, like a nice sorbet pink. Maybe they could've replaced all the rock/metal/grunge posters on the walls with a few nice framed pictures of kittens. Maybe there could've been a vase with scented roses at the cash desk, instead of the plastic skeleton-on-a-Harley-Davidson-motorbike that the scary/gorgeous guy was fiddling with while he talked on the phone.

But then I guess the people who wanted to shop here for second-hand albums, CDs and rare "comix" liked it just the way it was. They probably thought that it felt very authentic and gritty and real, even if – only two minutes down the road – everyone was strolling around eating 99s with raspberry sauce and comparing sunburn marks.

"But then he says to *me*, 'Yeah, but, Sigh, man – VSTs are old news. You want Audio Units plug-ins.'"

"Sigh"? The scary/gorgeous grunge boy was called "Sigh"? What was it with teenagers in this town and their weird nicknames? And speaking of people with weird nicknames, where was Deejay? I hadn't spotted him at all, but he *had* to be here, if Bob was impatiently waiting and "Howwww-ooooo!"ing outside.

As an old Nirvana track suddenly blasted through the shop's speakers, the top of someone's floppy head of fair hair started bouncing up and down in time behind the "M–R" alphabetized CD section. It was *him*, I was sure. But he was so short that I had to stand on my tiptoes and strain my neck just to see him properly. Which is when he saw *me*.

"Hi!" I saw Deejay mouth, over the bass-y boom of "Smells Like Teen Spirit".

"Hi!" I mouthed and waved shyly back, trying to lower myself down very slowly so that I looked more like a regular girl than a curly-haired, nosey-parker giraffe.

Help – he was walking over. Which is pretty much what I *wanted* to happen, but now I panicked about a) what to say to him, and b) whether I was going to say whatever I said to him with or *without* a stammer. . .

In the three seconds it took for him to reach me, I stuck what I hoped was a friendly smile on my face and did a quick inventory of Deejay: that floppy fair hair, still bouncing when he walked; a grin a mile wide; jeans and baseball boots; a faded grey T-shirt with the slogan "I'm with Stupid!" printed in dark blue with an arrow pointing to the right.

"Like the *X-Men*, do you?" he asked, nodding his head at the magazine I hadn't realized I was holding.

"Yes," I told him.

I hated the *X-Men*. Neisha made us watch the first one on DVD 'cause she's got this thing about

50

wanting to be Halle Berry, and I hated it so much that when she suggested we all go and see the follow-up, I told her I'd rather change both my brothers' nappies for a *month* than sit through another load of super-heroes with numpty names saving the planet or whatever *again*.

"I don't really like them," said Deejay, shrugging.

(Drat!)

"Did you see Nightcrawler in the *X-Men 2* movie?" he asked (I shook my head). "It was just a bloke with black face paint on! How's *that* meant to be scary? My mum looks scarier than that first thing in the morning!"

Listening to him, it dawned on me that Deejay maybe wasn't as young as I'd first thought. Close up, he looked and sounded maybe about thirteen, same as me. Maybe Deejay wasn't so much a kid and was just plain *short*.

"Howwww-ooooo!"

"Hey, I meant to ask you yesterday," said Deejay, casting a wary glance towards the door, where Bob's hairy face could be seen peering in. "Where've you moved from?"

"London. Kentish Town," I told him (where I used to be known for my stammer, I *didn't* tell him).

51

"Howwww-ooooo!"

"Yeah? Wow – this place must be pretty boring compared to London!"

Deejay sounded genuinely interested, but he couldn't help fidgeting at the sound of Bob's yowling.

"I dunno," I shrugged.

I hadn't planned on liking Portbay when I first arrived, but what I *did* like was that I could reinvent myself here; not have to be just Frankie's shy best friend, or hide me and my stammer behind all my other brilliant but loud girl mates. Course it would be handy to have someone to show my reinvented self off *to*. Auntie V always used to ask me how Frankie etc. were, just 'cause she could never remember (or be *bothered* to remember) Eleni, Parminder, Lauren and Neisha's names. And here in Portbay, I needed a new "etc.". Could Deejay be it?

"Howwww-ooooo!"

"Look, I'd better go – Bob'll be in here in a second, and Simon barred him after he peed on a pile of *Star Wars* box sets," said Deejay agitatedly. "Anyway, I've got to go and pick up my little sister."

"Oh, OK," I replied, half-taking in the fact that "Sigh" must be "Si" as in "Simon".

52

I was stupidly disappointed. Not about the scary/gorgeous guy having a less intriguing nickname than I'd thought, but disappointed about Deejay leaving five seconds into our conversation. I don't know what I'd hoped for exactly, but maybe I'd kind of *half*-hoped that me and him could hang out for a bit, and I could ask him stuff like *why* he was hiding from his mates yesterday and *why* a seagull had a grudge against him. Maybe I could have told him all about my friends back home, and how this shop reminded me of loads of stores and stalls in Camden Market near where I used to live, and maybe I could have even worked up to admitting that I'd lied about liking the *X-Men* and I didn't know why.

But Deejay was already heading out of the door, squeezing past a sulky girl in a black leather jacket, stripy black and purple tights, Doc Martens and – eek! – a pink tutu, who pushed past him like he wasn't even there (hey, he wasn't *that* small).

I nearly burst out laughing when I saw Deejay pull a face behind her back, but I didn't think that was a great idea, since she looked like she wasn't the sort of girl who could take a joke. (Hey, maybe if he'd stuck around I could've asked why so many girls in Portbay looked so sulky, *and* what that tutu was all about.)

"Uh. . ." Deejay called out, just before he stepped out of the gloom and into dazzling daylight. "You don't fancy meeting up tomorrow afternoon, do you? I could show you around . . . if you want!"

If I wanted? If I *wanted*? It was the exact, specific, *precise* thing I wanted more than anything. A mate to hang out with? Yes, please!

"Why not?" I said, deciding to play it cool and not come across as a desperate, clingy saddo.

"'Bout two o'clock, then? Down on the prom, by the water fountain?"

I had no idea where that was exactly, but that wasn't going to stop me.

"Sure!"

Deejay nodded in reply to my stupid, overeagerly nodding head, then waved as he and Bob sloped off together.

And then I realized that I knew Deejay and Bob's names, but they didn't know mine. Hey, perhaps I should have a go at reinventing my name before I met up with them tomorrow. I could call myself something cooler, like Halle, or Brodie or Courtney. . .

But it would kind of blow my cover if me and

Deejay (and Bob) *did* happen to become proper mates and my parents or my brothers called me by my real name in front of him. And anyway, I'd only recently managed to say it out loud without stumbling all over it.

Nope, tomorrow Stella Stansfield would be officially introducing herself to Deejay and Bob – and I couldn't *wait*. . .

CHAPTER 6

The 1% idiot factor

Mum and Dad were delirious.

They tried to pretend they weren't, but they *so* were.

I kind of wished I hadn't said *anything* about Deejay and meeting up with him tomorrow; they'd quizzed me so much about it all through tea that it had started to do my head in. I mean, I *know* they were excited about the idea of me having an actual, living, human friend in the town, but I was getting fed up with saying "I don't know", every time they asked questions like "How old is he?", "Where does he live?", "Do you think you'd like to invite him round here?", "Does he know how relieved and grateful we are?" (OK, so maybe I made that last one up. But I bet one, or more like *both* of them thought it.)

Thumpetty-thumpetty-thumpetty-DOOF.

After escaping from Mum and Dad and their well-meaning, we're-so-happy-for-you grins, I was now kneeling on the floor, staring out of my bedroom window, with only Peaches and the stars for company. I'd been thinking about how happy I was to have made a potential friend today, while Peaches had been contentedly purring, drooling and padding his claws into my knees. But both of us stopped thinking, drooling and clawing the second we heard that noise.

"It's like a riddle in a Christmas cracker, isn't it?" I whispered to Peaches, as though whoever (or whatever) lived in the house at the bottom of the garden could hear us, as much as we could hear them (it). "What goes *thumpetty-thumpetty-thumpetty-DOOF*? Only we don't know the answer. . ."

"Prrrrrp," prrrrrped Peaches, agreeing with me.

Though there was something I *did* know about the odd occupants of the place; when I'd come home this afternoon with no drawings but tales of Deejay, Mum had blurted out a snippet of info direct from our next-door-neighbour Maggie. She'd said nobody lived in that cottage permanently – it was just rented out to holidaymakers in the summer.

I squinted at the closed curtains, and tried to figure out what would have brought a family of sumo-wrestling poltergeists to Portbay. Couldn't they have stayed at *home* and rattled things? Maybe they just fancied a bit of sea air while they were swirling furniture around the room, you never know. . .

Bleep!

A text – great. Not that I could find my phone at first; it seemed to have a habit of wandering off this week.

"You found it for me yesterday, Fatso, so got any ideas today?" I asked Peaches, scrambling round my room and hoping it would bleep again so I could play a game of "You're getting hotter!" and track the stupid thing down.

Peaches yawned, his one, long yellow fang glinting by the light of the small lamp by my bed. (The small lamp was the best way to illuminate my room – overhead lights and full sun showed up the semi-stripped flowery wallpaper and lumpily plastered walls that were probably *last* on Dad's list of things to fix around here.)

At first I thought Peaches was turning his back on me and settling down for a snooze. Well, he *was*, but his tail was stretched out, straight as a furry arrow, flicking in the direction of my trainers. Since I didn't have anything else to go on, I thought I might as well try there, and sure enough, my mobile was nestling in one trainer, along with a blue Smartie and a Duplo brick. Looked like one or both of the twins had been in here while I was hanging out in The Vault this afternoon. . .

Hi Stell! Talked 2 Lauren yet? Got to ask about her nu piercing – ha! Wot u up 2? Lol Neish x.

Uh-oh, I winced, reading Neisha's text. I'd forgotten Lauren was going for that today. I didn't much like the sound of that "ha!".

Something must've gone wrong, I realized, about to phone Neisha straight back and ask. But then I stopped. It's just that if I got talking to Neish, she'd ask me what I was up to, and then I'd end up telling her about Deejay – and I wasn't sure I wanted to, not yet anyway. It's just that even though I hoped it would have got back to the others (via Lauren) about me being absolutely, honestly *fine* about Frankie and Seb, I still had a funny feeling they'd get overexcited, get the wrong idea about Deejay, and think he was a budding *boyfriend* or something. So I copped out and texted Neisha back (*"Wot happened? Tell, tell!"*), and decided I'd go downstairs soon and drop Lauren an e-mail to see what was going on with that tummy button of hers.

I guess this holding back on talking about Deejay had something to do with Frankie's mum.

Frankie's mum – otherwise known as Aunt Esme, otherwise known as my ex-childminder – used to love spilling her pearls of wisdom my way, mainly 'cause if she tried it on her own daughter, Frankie tended to roll her eyes and shake her head. But one of Aunt Esme's sayings had come into my head now: "Stella, my sweetheart, 99% of the time, you got to trust your instincts. But always hold back till you check for that 1%. . ."

Well, 99% of me had a good feeling about Deejay, and only 1% worried that I'd got it wrong and he was an idiot. So until I met up with him tomorrow and sussed out whether he was an idiot or not, I'd do like Aunt Esme said and hold back on telling any of my friends back in London about him, before they'd practically married me off to him, just like Mum and Dad had done. . .

"*La, la, la, la, la-LA-LAHHHHHH!*" a megaphone-loud voice boomed from somewhere across the lane, jarring me out of my thoughts.

OK, that was it. I didn't care whether Deejay was a solid gold ace person or a nutter; as long as he owned a pair of binoculars he was prepared to lend to me, I'd be his friend for *life*. . .

CHAPTER 7

I must have made a mistook

"Oh, hi!" I smiled shyly.

"Hiya!" grinned Deejay, surprising me by coming up to the water fountain via the beach, while I'd been glancing nervously up and down the prom for him.

"Hurrrufff!" said Bob, stopping to scratch some sand out of his huge ear with a mighty rear paw.

"D'you fancy walking along by the harbour?" he asked (Deejay, I mean, not Bob).

"Yeah, sure," I said with a nod, not wanting to admit that I didn't even know that Portbay *had* a harbour. I'd only explored what lay beyond one end of the beach (Sugar Bay). I'd never gone very far along in the other direction.

"I mean, I know it smells of fish and everything, but there're these winding stairs there that take you up to the main road and the crazy golf. That's like, if you *fancy* playing crazy golf."

"Yeah! That's fine!" I told him.

61

I knew the Crazy Golf course – me and Frankie had passed it on Saturday. It was all themed like something out of *Pirates of the Caribbean*, which I thought looked fun, but Frankie decided was naff. So we hadn't gone in.

"I'm Stella, by the way," I said, suddenly remembering that Deejay still didn't know this one vital piece of information about me.

"I'm TJ," said, er, Deejay.

Oops. . .

It was a simple case of mistaken identity. Or looking at it another way, it was me being a berk and getting it all wrong. Again.

The thing is, when I get nervous – apart from stressing about stammering – I tend to mishear things. Like at primary school, when I got summoned to the headteacher's office this one time. With the blood thudding at breakneck speed through my panicked head (what had I *done?*), I could have *sworn* she'd shouted, "Come in!" when I knocked on her door. It was only when I barged into her office and caught her flossing sweetcorn out of her teeth that I realized she'd said, "Coming!" (It turned out that she'd called for me so she could tell me one of my pictures had been entered for a local art competition. Bet she wished she could withdraw it after that. . .)

And last week, I'd got the name of the prom café wrong (it was called the Shingle café, not "Shingles", as in the disease, though I'd never stop thinking of it that way). And *then* I'd got the name of the old mansion at Sugar Bay wrong; I thought it was called the Josephs' house, and guessed that was the name of the rich family who'd built it. But it's actually called *Joseph's* house, in honour of Joseph, the young black servant boy who came back with the family from Barbados, where they'd had sugar plantations, back in eighteen-hundred-and-something-or-other.

Then yesterday in The Vault, there was that whole, dumb Sigh/Si/Simon muddle in my head.

So I'd made another mistook and got yet *another* name wrong; what was new?

"*Tee*jay?" I said, frowning and slightly flustered, as we strolled along the prom.

"TJ – just the initials 'T' and 'J'."

"Oh! I . . . I thought it was something else. . ."

"Like what?" TJ asked, padding along beside me in his baseball boots, his head just coming up to my shoulders.

"I, um, wasn't sure," I said, waffling a bit and trying not to make too much of a fool of myself in front of my potential new friend (and his dog, who was tagging along by his side, like a big hairy minder). "Those guys shouting at you on the beach on Monday ... I couldn't figure out properly what they were calling you."

"Well, it was *kind* of a miracle that they were using my proper name," he shrugged, his hands thrust deep in his jeans pockets. "Normally, they just call me Titch, or Lofty. Or Knee-high. Or Bug."

"Huh? But I thought they were your friends?" I said, horrified to hear that roll call of nasty nicknames.

"Uh, *sort* of. They never used to bother with me, but they've been getting more matey recently. Dunno why ... but I s'pose it's good, 'cause they're a couple of years older than me, and they're kind of *cool* at my school. But sometimes they're a bit, well, *y'know*. If you see what I mean."

Yes – straight away I was pretty sure I did know, even if TJ wasn't explaining himself in a sparklingly clear way. I guessed that he meant that he was flattered that a gang of older, cocky, tough lads were paying him any attention. But he was also pretty wary of them; you could tell that from the way he was speaking about them just now, and from his body language on Monday (i.e. when he tried to use me as a human shield).

"How old are they anyway?" I asked, realizing this could be a subtle way to solve the mystery of just how old TJ was.

"Sam, Ben and Marcus are fifteen. I think Aiden might be sixteen now."

Fifteen . . . he'd already said they were a couple of years older, so that made TJ thirteen, same as me. He was just straightforward *short*, then.

"I saw you . . . well, I think I *almost* saw you later, down on the sands – you were right in the middle of those lads," I told him. "Your dog and your sister were following behind you."

"Yeah, they were just fooling around. Said they fancied playing beach volleyball, and I could be the ball. . ."

At first I thought TJ was joking, since he seemed to be a smiley, jokey kind of person. But I realized that although he *did* have a frozen-looking smile in place, he must've been pretty humiliated by the volleyball jibe, from the way he was examining the cracks in the pavement so intently.

Hey, maybe it was a good time to change the subject.

"So . . . what does TJ stand for then?"

"Nothing, not any more!" he said with a shrug. "I've just been TJ for forever. *Everyone* just calls me TJ. Even teachers."

"But it must stand for something! Thomas James?" I guessed, thinking of the most common names I knew that started with those letters.

"Nah," said TJ, shaking his head and grinning.

"Toby Joshua?"

"*Toby!* Give me a break!" he laughed.

"OK, OK. Well, how about. . ." I tried to think of the fanciest, most fanciful name I could come up with. ". . .I know! Tarquin Jethro!"

This was fun; having someone to fool around with. It was only when I noticed TJ doing that crack-in-the-pavement staring thing again that I realized he might *not* be having fun.

"You're not *really* called Tarquin Jethro, are you?" I asked, hoping I hadn't put my foot in it and guessed his actual name at the same time as taking the mickey out of it.

"No," said TJ, with a shake of his head, his floppy hair falling round his face. "It's just plain TJ."

We'd been hanging out for all of three minutes and already I was wondering if my 99% gut reaction had been totally wrong. I mean, TJ had gone from grinning to gloomy to grinning to gloomy again.

I tried to think of something to say that might get the grinning version back again, but I was suddenly so nervous that I worried that anything

66

I might try and say would have a stammer at the beginning of it. So I shut up.

Cool way to start a new friendship, huh?

Above us, under a baby blue cloudless sky, a life-size plastic palm tree flapped its fronds in the sea breeze.

TJ had one elbow leaning on the beak of a luminous pink flamingo (fake), and was doing his best to put me off.

"You've got *no* chance."

"Wrong!" I said, tightening my grip around the club and aiming for the pirate's head. "Bet you a bag of chips I can get it in his mouth!"

"Bet you a bag of chips with onion rings you *can't*!"

Phew. I still didn't quite understand what had gone on when we first met up earlier, but I was having a *way* better time hanging out with TJ now. After strolling through the harbour (v picturesque, v fishy, v sure I spotted Peaches sitting on a boat washing his scruffy fur. . .), we'd ended up as planned at the Treasure Island crazy golf, and so far we were neck and neck, taking about fifty trillion putts to get about three-quarters of the way around the course. Me and TJ, it turned out, were both *equally* rubbish crazy golfers, and were having a *ball* being so rubbish. The only one who *didn't* seem to be enjoying the afternoon was Bob, who kept peering mournfully over the perimeter hedge, watching our every move, guilt-tripping us into remembering that dogs were (most cruelly) not allowed in Treasure Island.

"Urgh!"

That was me, groaning as my ball ricocheted off the pirate's nose.

"Ha ha ha!" cackled TJ, doing a quick victory dance at the side of me. "One order of chips and onion rings, please, with plenty of salt 'n' vinegar!"

Grinning grimly, I glanced over at the takeaway van parked outside the entrance. Perched on top of it, I noticed, was a large seagull, staring intently our way. I decided not to mention it to TJ – there was no point getting him wound up, if it was just any old gull, and not the dive-bombing nutter-bird. And who wanted to spoil a great afternoon now? Not me.

Actually, we had Lauren to thank for getting us over that bumpy start earlier – not that she *knew* it. While we were walking along in silence, she'd texted me to tell me *today's* bad news: that not only was yesterday's belly-button piercing lopsided

68

(thanks to her screaming and jumping at the wrong moment), but now it had gone septic too. After I read that out to TJ, I'd gone on to explain my disastrous attempts to cheer Lauren up when we were e-mailing last night. When I told him I'd written *"Hey, it's OK – maybe you'll start a new fashion for squint piercings!"*, he'd laughed so much he got hiccups and kind of frightened Bob.

After that, *nothing* got in the way of us talking like we'd known each other for ever, rushing to fill in the details of our lives. *I* told him about Mum and Dad and the twins, and how I had to help look after them; *he* told me about his mum (an actress) and his kid sister Ellie (the little blonde singing girl) and how he had to look after her a *lot* of the time. *I* told him how much I'd hated the idea of moving from London to here, but how OK I felt about it now; *he* told me about the school I'd be starting at, and said it was "all right". *I* told him about Frankie and the other friends I'd left behind in Kentish Town; *he* told me how he got on with loads of people at school, but wasn't close to anyone in particular, since they *all* took digs at him about his height. *I* talked to him about Sugar Bay; *he* told me him and Bob walked over there all the time. *I* asked him if he knew any of the weirdos I'd come across in the town so far;

he told me he wasn't sure about Mrs Sticky Toffee (but hey – what thirteen-year-old boy is interested in bizarre old ladies?), but he certainly knew the tap-dancing librarian I'd spotted stamping out the books in the library last week – he was TJ's sister's Saturday morning tap and jazz dance teacher.

I sucked in all the information like I was a girl-shaped sponge. Course, there was *other* stuff I wasn't so keen to hear: like the sniggering café crew down on the beach? Well, TJ said their names were Rachel, Brooke, Hazel and Kayleigh, they were totally in love with themselves, and were the main clique in what would be my year at school (oh, *great*). The one I'd seen hovering at the door of the Portbay Nafferia was Rachel, apparently – her mum owned the shop (and was responsible for all that bad taste craft tat, then).

"Right! Move over!" said TJ, nudging me out of the way and getting ready to take his aim at the pirate's mouth.

"Yeah, yeah, Tiger Woods!" I goaded him, using the name of the *one* golfer in the world I'd actually ever heard of.

Just as TJ was about to take aim, there was a swoosh of air, a flap of gigantic wings, and a large seagull pooped *right* in front of the toe of TJ's left baseball boot.

So, it *was* the same gull with a grudge.

"What's that bird got against you?" I asked, watching as it soared skyward, whirling impossibly high on some unseen current of air.

"I whacked it with a pebble once," said TJ, glancing up warily in the air.

"You did *what*?"

To tell the truth, I was kind of *shocked* to hear him admitting a case of animal cruelty so easily.

"Not *deliberately*, Stella!" said TJ, turning and staring appealingly at me. "I was out at Sugar Bay a couple of months ago with Bob, and I was just skimming stones off the waves. And then one of the stones pinged off a big hunk of rock, and – *blam!* – it hits this seagull flying past. . ."

"What – and it's had it in for you ever since?" I asked, incredulous.

"Uh-huh. Every time I come down near the sea, it goes for me, and—"

Midway through his sentence, TJ caught sight of something. The something happened to be the digital clock fixed on the side of the lookey-likey Spanish Armada galleon where you bought your crazy golf tickets and hired your clubs.

"Urgh – I didn't realize it was that *late*!" he

mumbled, shoving his golf club at me. "I've got to run – I was supposed to pick up Ellie ten minutes ago!"

"Um . . . you don't fancy coming round to mine tomorrow, do you?" I heard a confident-ish voice shout out after him. (Oo-er, it was mine!)

"What time?" he called out, skipping backwards towards the entrance.

"One-ish?"

"Yeah! Sounds OK! See you then, Stella!"

And with the briefest of "see you!"s, TJ took off like (a short) Cinderella, even though the clock on the galleon had just struck ten past four, and not midnight; and even though Cinderella didn't tend to be pictured in the fairy-tale books wearing jeans, baseball boots and a Strokes T-shirt.

"See you!" I smiled, as I watched my new best friend dash off, followed by a galumphing great dog and a low-flying, slow-flapping seagull. . .

The amazing, inflatable cat

Once upon a time, long, long ago, Elize Grainger would have sat in her tiny studio (now my den), gazing out of the small window at her prettily planted garden (now our jungle).

Taking a break from working on the flower fairy watercolours she did so well (like the one I'd hung on the wall), the elderly Elize would take a sip of tea from her delicate, rose-patterned china cup (now dusted off and displayed on one of my shelves) and muse over the faraway days of her childhood. There were those hazy memories of running wild on her parents' plantation in Barbados, followed by happy times in the Big House in Sugar Bay, with the family's trusty servant and her best friend Joseph to keep her company on long walks along the beaches of Portbay. . .

Between exploring the old mansion, finding stuff when I was clearing the den, mooching around the museum, and getting a copy of an old local paper from our neighbour, I'd pieced together plenty about Elize Grainger's life, and vaguely imagined the rest. But I wondered what she'd think if she could gaze around her old studio now. Maybe she'd be thrilled that I'd restored it a little. Maybe she'd be chuffed to see her own knick-knacks displayed. Maybe she'd be pleased that another artist (i.e. me) was following in her footsteps, even if I wasn't sure what she'd make of *my* take on fairies (i.e. the funkier the better). One thing was for sure, I don't think she'd have taken too kindly to having a farting dog slobbing out on the floor. . .

"Oh, God! I'm sorry!" said TJ, wincing and flapping his hand in front of his face. "I ran out of his dog biscuits this morning and had to give him a tin of tuna instead. It *always* does that to him."

A sprawled Bob snoozed on, unaware of the whiff he'd just caused.

"It's OK – I've got two little brothers, remember?" I told TJ, wafting the den door back and forward to let some air in. "You need a gas mask when you're changing their nappies sometimes!"

"You'd need to give me a gas mask and a million pounds before I'd go near a dirty nappy!"

74

said TJ with a wicked grin, as he turned his attention to my corkboard. "Hey, look at that – did you do this?"

"Yeah," I nodded, feeling a bit shy as he studied my best attempt at a modern-day fairy. "I like a lot of Japanese animation and stuff. . ."

"A ninja fairy – cool!" he grinned, studying the mutant butterfly wings and big dewy eyes I'd drawn on the little figure. "She looks sort of like your mum!"

I hadn't thought of it that way, but I guess my mum *did* have a pixieish face, specially with her new haircut.

Speaking of Mum, I thought she'd been very restrained when TJ had turned up a little while ago, with Ellie and Bob in tow. I'd been sure she was going to throw her arms around him and give him some reward money for being friends with me, but instead she'd just smiled a lot and forced tonnes of biscuits on him, which hopefully came across as being in the normal range of mum-ly behaviour. (Thank goodness Dad was away choosing toilets or whatever at the plumber's yard; he'd probably have mortified me by asking TJ to be an honorary member of the Stansfield family or something.)

"And you did that too?" he asked, pointing to a

cartoon drawing of two girls, one with huge ears, one with a huge nose.

"Yeah – those are two of my friends from London; Lauren and Eleni. Eleni thought it was pretty funny, but Lauren wasn't too chuffed with it!" I explained, stepping closer and gazing over TJ's shoulder (and head) at the caricature, and at the board pinned full of bits of my life. "And that's Frankie."

"Yeah, I know."

Er. . .

How *exactly* could TJ know that the mad-looking girl fooling around in the photo-booth strip of snaps was Frankie? I mean, *yeah*, so I'd talked about her yesterday, but. . .

"Poo! Smelly!" said TJ's kid sister, appearing in the doorway and doing a quick mini tap-dance on the worn, flat doorstep. "Do you know something? Because my name is Ellie, I get called 'Smelly' at school sometimes, but only by boys, and *they're* smelly. Aren't they?"

Before I had a chance to answer, Ellie broke into another tap move and another snatch of conversation.

"Was this someone's little house? It *looks* like it was someone's little house. It's nice but it's a bit dark. You could paint it a bright colour!

What's your favourite colour? Mine is lilac. That's a proper colour; that's a kind of purple. *And* it's a plant. My mummy said she nearly called me Lilac when I was born, which would have been good, 'cause it wouldn't have rhymed with 'smelly'."

Yeah, but the smelly boys at school *sure* would have had a field day teasing her about having a name like Lilac. . .

"Hey, Ellie – I thought you were supposed to be playing with Stella's little brothers?" said TJ, widening his eyes enthusiastically.

As an older sibling, I could tell straight away that TJ had just spoken in code. What he'd *actually* said was: "I like you a lot, Ellie, but you are doing my head in. Please, *please* go away."

"Yes, but I just came out to say hello! So hello! And bye*eeee*!" trilled Ellie, spinning around on her pink and white trainers and bouncing towards the house.

"She's cute!" I said, as soon as she'd skipped out of hearing range.

"Yeah, cute as a migraine!"

"That bad?" I laughed.

"Well, *you* try getting woken up by her singing along to her *Lion King* video at twenty to seven in the morning!"

"Today, you mean? Or every day?"

"*Every* day," sighed TJ, flopping down on the chair by the desk, like he was exhausted by the very memory. "I mean, it's the holidays, isn't it? But Ellie's always been the same; the *milli*second she's awake, she's up and doing stuff. With me, it takes about an hour just to get both my eyelids to move up and down at the same time. . ."

"And has she always been into the dancing and stuff?"

"Uh-huh. She sings along to ads on the telly, and tap-dances to the theme tune of every programme going. Soaps, the news, weather jingles, whatever."

"Does it drive your mum mad too?" I asked, stretching my leg out and ruffling Bob's fur with my bare foot. TJ hadn't mentioned a dad so far, and I hadn't liked to ask.

"Are you kidding?" said TJ, as his eyes drifted along the rows of trinkets (a few of mine, a few of Elize's) that I had stashed on the shelves of the den. "If you want an idea of what my mum's like, just think of Ellie . . . but aged 36."

"What – she dances along to the weather report too?"

"Near enough! Like I told you, she does all this amateur dramatic stuff, so she's always wandering

78

around, rehearsing her lines or belting out some dumb song."

She'd been a proper actress in London, TJ's mum: he'd said so yesterday, when we'd been swapping life stories, on the way to the crazy golf. She'd been an extra in *Coronation Street* and was the star in a commercial for cheese and everything. That was before TJ was born, before she moved to Portbay. And nowadays, his mum was involved in so many local acting groups and ran so many workshops that TJ ended up with Ellie skipping and singing after him a lot of the time.

"Yeah, but you get on with your mum, right?"

As I spoke, Bob rolled over sleepily and let me rub his tummy with my foot.

"She's OK," said TJ, looking faintly gloomy for a second. "It just bugs me that *one* minute she thinks I'm grown-up and responsible enough to look after Ellie, and the next minute she's babying me like I'm a cross between a six year old and a chihuahua!"

I nearly sniggered, but however much TJ *did* look like an adorable puppy, I could tell pretty well by now that his height was a real issue. I needed to say the right thing, to tell him he wasn't *that* short and didn't look anything like a cute little dog (both lies). But before I could work out the right words to say, a fat cat squished its way through the one empty square pane in the den window.

Uh-oh, I thought, glancing down at Bob.

"Uh-oh," said TJ out loud, thinking the same thing as me.

Unfortunately, clocking some different tone in his master's voice, Bob raised a hairy head, eyes inquisitive and tongue lolling.

Peaches – spotting Bob – stopped dead, his one yellow fang glinting ominously. I couldn't breathe, I couldn't move. Then the weirdest thing happened: Peaches inflated.

Ever seen one of those spiky blowfish, that fill up with air like a prickly balloon the minute trouble swims on to the horizon? There's one in the film *Finding Nemo* – if Jamie had been in here, he'd have been giggling and clapping his hands at Peaches' furry puffy efforts.

"Wow. . ." murmured TJ, well impressed by my cat's alarming and intimidating size. Bob, meanwhile, just looked cowed and confused, his ears flattened to his head like someone had Sellotaped them there.

Then, just as quickly as he'd inflated, Peaches let all the air fizz out of his fur or wherever the heck it was hidden, and slipped down into his normal, scruffy fat cat proportions. Just as slowly, Bob's ears rose up to their usual position, only twitching very slightly. I don't know whether it was just a show of strength, or if Peaches had actually *hypnotized* Bob, but one thing was for certain; Bob wouldn't be leaping and barking at His Tubbiness any time soon. In fact, ever-faithful Bob didn't even *dare* make a fuss when Peaches casually waddled over to TJ via the desk and plopped himself comfily down on to his lap.

TJ and me, we stared at each other, eyebrows raised, not exactly sure what we'd just witnessed. We were so taken with Peaches' powers, that we both jumped when we heard Mum's voice.

"I see the sumo-wrestling poltergeists are at it again!" she said, standing in the doorway grinning, a basket of clean laundry on her hip, all ready to hang out. Behind her, in the jungle we laughingly called the garden, Ellie was spinning round in a circle with Jamie, singing "Ring-a-ring-o-roses", to the accompaniment of a distant CLANG!-*boiiinng*- CLANG!-*boiiinng*- CLANG!-*boiiinng*. . .

"Huh?" huh-ed TJ, glancing back and forth between me and Mum as he tried to figure out what she'd meant.

"The people in the holiday house over the lane," I began to explain. "They're making all these weird noises – we can't figure out what they're up to!"

A little light went on in TJ's eyes at the mention of that mystery; the same sort of light that flicks on when you tell a boy that you know where he can get free tickets for top seats to see his favourite football team play. When I spotted that, I felt a little thrill; maybe me and TJ could investigate the noises together? That could be a laugh. And after all, he *did* look a little bit like Shaggy out of *Scooby-Doo*, only half the size. . .

Then the moment was gone, with Jake whirling into the den like a chubby thigh-high whirlwind, coming to a crashing halt at TJ's knees.

"Oof!" TJ laughed. "Well, thank you! What's this?"

As soon as TJ picked up the thing Jake had dumped in his lap, half draping it over Peaches' head, I knew I wanted to die.

"Stella *pants*!" said Jake, smiling happily, as his new friend examined the lovely gift – freshly stolen from the laundry basket – that he'd been handed.

Great.

There's nothing like having your pink dotty knickers held in the air by your new – BOY – mate to make a girl deflate like a furry blowfish. . .

CHAPTER 9

Surviving the pants trauma

If anyone had been peeking in the bathroom right now, they'd . . .

a) be a bit pervy, and

b) probably assume that I was trying to drown myself out of sheer shame.

But I *wasn't* trying to drown myself, honest – even if the memory of TJ holding up my knickers to the world this afternoon still made me feel faintly sick. TJ seemed pretty mortified too, even though he tried to crack a joke about it at the time and put my knickers on Jake's head. The fact that he announced he had to go home about two seconds later was a pretty *big* clue that he was embarrassed, after all. . .

Anyway, another reason I definitely wasn't drowning myself was that there was too much distracting *noise* going on around here.

THUD-a-dud-a-dud-a-dud.

THUD-a-dud-a-dud-a-dud.

THUD-a-dud-a-dud-a-dud.

With my head tilted back, everything from my nose downwards was underwater. That included my ears, but somehow I could still make out those mysterious loud thuds (and duds) that had been radiating from the house at the bottom of the garden for the last half-hour.

THUD-a-dud-a-dud-a-dud.

Although Mum and Dad were pretending to mind their own business, I could tell all the unexplained racket was starting to get to them – when I'd left them downstairs earlier, they were tutting and turning up the volume on the *Channel Four News*.

"Ah . . . *whooof!*"

Now *that* was a new noise. A faraway, high-pitched, girlish barking sort of noise.

"Ah . . . *whooof!*"

And there it was again. I was quite comfy, submerged among the bubbles, but curiosity got the better of me. Slowly, I raised my head out of the water, and tilted it to one side to listen better, letting water dribble out of my ear at the same time.

"Ah . . . *whooof!*"

You know what? That *wasn't* a faraway, high-pitched, girlish bark – that was a nearby, high-pitched, cattish *sneeze*.

"Oh, hello!" I said to Peaches, who I spotted unexpectedly curled up on the closed toilet seat, delicately achoo-ing. "I thought you were doing an impersonation of Bob there!"

"Ah . . . *whooof!*" sneezed Peaches again.

It was the talc that was doing it, I think. A fine layer of powdery-ness covered most of the surfaces in the room, as a little reminder that it had been bath-time mayhem with the boys in here not so long ago.

But they were safely stashed in their cots now, and it was *my* turn to have the place to myself. I was making the most of it – mainly 'cause the bath wouldn't be here from tomorrow.

The old, worn, damp-smelly carpet, wall tiles and even the sink had already gone – turfed in the overflowing skip out in the driveway – and tomorrow, they'd be followed by the bath and the loo. Dad had promised that our shiny new bathroom suite (currently parked outside the front door, smothered in industrial-strength bubble wrap) would be all in place by the end of the day, but I wasn't going to bank on it.

So here I was, making like a prune, soaking in water that was so deep that if I wafted my little finger, a mini tidal wave would go slooshing over the edge. Does it sound like I was having a nice, relaxing time? Well, I *wasn't*, and it had nothing to do with the background thudding and sneezing, *or* today's pants trauma. . .

"I think I need to talk to someone," I mumbled, turning and staring at Peaches, and creating a major flood at the same time. "I should phone Frankie, shouldn't I?"

Despite the fact that in his feline wisdom, Peaches must have decided to come through and keep me company, he didn't respond at all to what I'd just said. Course, why should I have expected him to? He was only a cat. But then, in the short time I'd known Peaches, I'd begun to suspect that he wasn't your average Felix-eating, purr-rumbling moggy. For a start, he might have *looked* like a scruff, but I didn't know any other pet that wafted a trail of peaches and cream when they left a room. Then there was his habit of turning up where you least expected him; which was just *one* of Peaches' many psychic pussy traits. So the fact that he just started licking his bottom when I mentioned Frankie sort of threw me.

"Er . . . what about Eleni, then? She's always up for a chat."

[Lick, lick, lick. . .]

"Well, Parminder? She's pretty sensible."

[Lick, lick, lick. . .]

"Lauren? I mean, I know she's a bit *dippy*. . ."

[Lick, lick, lick. . .]

"Neisha?"

[Lick, lick, lick. . .]

This was *mad*: I was basing my decision on who to call and splurge out my troubles to on whether a cat would stop licking its bum or not. But whatever; I had one last name on my mind.

"Auntie V?"

Instantly, Peaches abandoned his bottom and stared straight at me.

"Prrrp!"

It was only a small noise, and just as instantly, Peaches turned back to continue his wash-and-brush-up, but it made up my mind for me.

(I tell you, my friends back in London would think I'd gone *mad*. . .)

"*One* minute," I explained, pressing my mobile against my ear, like that would make my call somehow more private, "they were all gaga about TJ: Dad was going on and *on* about how sorry he was to have missed meeting him, and Mum was totally *raving* about how nice he was. . ."

I was scrunched up on my bed, wrapped in a towel with a cat asleep on my feet, having a low-voiced moan to Auntie V about the conversation at teatime tonight. The one that began with Mum and Dad practically offering to start up the TJ Fan Club, and finished with them acting like they expected to see him popping up on *Crimewatch* later.

". . .but then I said to Mum, 'Oh, remember those boys that were sniggering at me in the Shingles café, that first time me and you and the twins went in there?', and Mum said yeah, and then *I* said, 'Well, TJ's been hanging out with them. They're a bit tough and I don't think he really likes them that much, but I think he's just doing it 'cause he's got this chip on his shoulder about being small, and a bit of him's chuffed that they're paying him attention.'"

"Let me guess. . ." Auntie V suggested drily. "Suddenly they're not smiling quite so brightly?"

"Too right," I said, nodding – not that Auntie V could see that. "They just sort of gave each other this *look*, and then Dad said to me, 'You mean he's in a *gang*?' And I just thought, uh-oh. They're not going to have a *downer* on him, are they?"

"And I take it they do?"

"Oh, yeah. It's like, I tried telling them the lads weren't exactly a *gang*, and TJ wasn't *properly* hanging out with them, but they didn't look too chuffed. And they basically stopped talking about him."

"Hmm. . ." Auntie V sighed dramatically. I *bet* she was rolling her eyes. "The thing is, Stella my little star, I guess it's a parent's duty to be protective. I'm sure they get a rulebook the day their child is born and it says something like '*Rule 10: Be overprotective to the point where you drive your kids mad.*'"

That made me smile; that was exactly what I needed to hear. Peaches had been absolutely right about choosing Auntie V to blow off steam to. Honestly, I wouldn't have thought of her straight away, if I'd had to make up my mind on my own, without the help of a cat and its bum. I mean, I'd always got on pretty *well* with Auntie V, even if she did overwhelm me a bit by being a) gorgeous, b) sarcastic, c) dripping in confidence. But I'd never, *ever* had a heart-to-heart with her. Sure, when Mum and Dad were originally talking about moving to Portbay, I was more than happy to listen to Auntie V *snorting* at the very idea, while I nodded silently in the background. But tonight she was being totally brilliant, and hadn't sounded the *least* bit surprised when she'd picked up the phone and heard my moaning voice at the other end.

"And the thing is, Stella, one of the reasons your parents wanted to move to that dullsville little town you're stuck in was because they wanted to bring you and your brothers up somewhere they thought was safer."

Auntie V tended to refer to Portbay as "dullsville" because the idea of leaving London and its theatres and cinemas and shops and sushi bars was as nuts to Auntie V as volunteering to strap fish fingers to yourself and jump in a shark tank.

"But that's such a joke!" I blurted out, feeling defensive about my old home. "I never had any hassle in London!"

It was true; I wasn't sure exactly what my mum and dad were worried about, but back in Kentish Town, I didn't hang out with *anyone* in a gang; I'd *never* been mugged; nobody'd *ever* tried to offer me drugs. . . The closest I'd got to a real criminal was Eleni's cousin Georgiou, who got fined for being caught without a ticket on the tube once.

"*Tell* me about it, darling!" said Auntie V, laughing in that throaty voice of hers. "I mean, when I think about what your dad got up to in that so-called sleepy Norfolk village where we grew up, now *that's* the joke!"

What my dad got *up* to! What did she *mean* by that? I immediately thought of all the kiddie photos Granny and Grandad Stansfield showed

91

us when we visited; millions of snaps of two gangly blonde kids waving at the camera, playing in paddling pools, mucking about on a tree-swing.

"Why? What was my dad like?"

"He hasn't told you? About the trouble he got in to when he was fifteen?" Auntie V asked incredulously.

"*No* . . . what happened?"

"Well, if he hasn't told you, I'm not really at liberty to say. . . But all I *will* say is, if he gives you any trouble about your little friend PJ, just you turn round and ask him to tell you about the paintballing incident."

I couldn't let her get away with that; she *had* to tell me more. I was about to launch into a full-on begging session (not even bothering to correct TJ's name), when she called a sudden halt to the conversation.

"Oh, Stella, there's a call waiting on the line – I've got to go. It's this awful actor client of mine; he'll be phoning to see if I've heard anything about the beans commercial he tried out for today. And how am I going to break it to him that the director said he didn't make a very convincing bean? Anyway, call me any time, Stella – I mean it! Bye!"

So my dad had a deep, dark secret to do with

paintballing. What could he have done: splatted the side of a tractor, or a haystack or something? I might be dying of curiosity, but like Auntie V had suggested, I knew I should shelve that snippet of info and use it as ammunition if Dad or Mum got funny about TJ again. And even if they didn't, I could spring the paintballing question on him sometime, just for fun.

"Anyway, they're wrong about TJ, aren't they?" I whispered to Peaches, watching one ear flick in his sleep. "He's not some teen thug, is he?"

(Two flicks of the ear.)

"He could be a really good friend, eh, Peaches?"

(One flick.)

"Like me and you?"

(One flick.)

One flick for yes, two flicks for no.

There was one slightly mad, but completely true thing I'd learned since I'd been in Portbay: *always* trust a weird, scruffy, one-fanged fat cat that smells of peaches and cream.

Hey! I'd made up my first saying! Frankie's mum would be proud of me. . .

Chapter 10

Hark; a not-so-good noise

Frankie: mouthy, sassy, loyal as a loyal thing. Eleni: honest, upfront, brainy without showing off about it. Parminder: super-cool, super-cute, someone to look up to. Neisha: kooky, kind, kind of adorable. Lauren: ditzy, dreamer, total dipstick.

In a nutshell, that's what my old mates in my old neighbourhood were like. Not that you could tell any of that from the photos they'd just sent me: in the photo-booth strip I was gazing at, they looked like a bunch of hyperactive six year olds out to make the *Guinness Book of Records* for the Daftest Face Pulled In A Confined Space.

I was feeling much better this morning. The letter (and the photos) from the girls had really brightened my day, and last night's conversation with Auntie V had been pretty cool at reassuring me about TJ too. Peaches had been totally right to steer me in her direction (sort of); after all, *she* was the one who first came out with the phrase

"Stella etc.", putting the thought in my head that that an "etc." was *exactly* what I needed to help me feel at home in Portbay.

"What's that?" asked Dad, suddenly peering over my shoulder.

"Frankie and the girls," I explained, holding up the photo-booth strip for him to see, and pointing (pointlessly, as it turned out) at the envelope it had come in, which Jake had grabbed and was now using to stir the Ricicles around in his bowl.

"Yeah, but what's *that*?"

"Lauren's new belly-button piercing."

She'd got so close to the camera that her pink tummy was fuzzily out of focus. But you could still make out the silver hoop – and the fact that it wasn't what you might call dead-centre. . .

"Ah, what a laugh. Now *there's* the perfect friends for a girl to have, eh?" said Dad a little too brightly, squeezing my shoulders.

OK. So by that remark, Dad could mean one of three things. . .

1) Frankie, Eleni, Parminder, Neisha and Lauren were the perfect friends a girl could have.

2) Frankie, Eleni, Parminder, Neisha and Lauren were the perfect friends a girl could have, and I must miss them really badly.

3) Frankie, Eleni, Parminder, Neisha and

95

Lauren were the perfect friends a girl could have, and a no-good boy who hung out with the local gang wasn't any kind of friend in comparison.

I had a funny feeling that in his own, not-very-subtle way, Dad was guilty of the third option, which made me bristle a bit and think about hitting him with the paintballing question. . .

"So, what's everyone's plans for the day, then?" Dad asked, pulling out a chair and sitting down at the kitchen table along with me, Mum and the boys. "Whatever they are, I hope they don't include going for a wee, because I'm just about to dismantle the loo!"

As he said that, Dad grinned around the table, but especially aimed his beaming smile at me. I think he was hoping for a beaming smile in return, but all I managed was a half-hearted twitch at the corners of my mouth.

"Well, I'm taking the boys to the Little Acorns Play Workshop this morning, so we'll be safely out of your way!" Mum answered Dad, while wiping margarine off Jamie's eyebrows with a piece of kitchen roll.

The Little Acorns thing: that was one of the notices me and Mum had seen in the window of the Portbay Nafferia on the prom a few days ago.

"And Stella? What're *you* up to today?" asked

96

Dad, turning his cheery 100-watt beam of a grin my way again.

"Going to mug old ladies with TJ the Thug," I was tempted to say.

"Going drawing," I lied instead. We might not be planning on mugging old ladies, but before TJ had bolted yesterday afternoon, we'd vaguely arranged to text each other and maybe meet up today (and not mention the pants trauma, hopefully). Anyway, I didn't fancy telling my parents that, not after the way they'd cooled towards him.

But *urgh* . . . I had a funny feeling that my eyes were showing me up for the liar I was ("Big fat fibber!" they probably flashed). Luckily, Mum and Dad were temporarily distracted from my giveaway expression as they both rushed to stop Jake from eating the envelope from Frankie etc.

"Are you going drawing down at the beach?" Mum asked me, half-harassed, as Jamie tried to bite her outstretched arm.

"Mmmm," I mumbled, thinking that a vague "mmm" was less of a troublesome lie than a definite, truth-free "yes". . .

The ancient, brown, felt Victorian bonnet had lain unloved and undiscovered in the outhouse for a zillion years (OK, nearly eight decades, which was *practically* a zillion years, whichever way you looked at it).

Then I'd found it, dusted it off, and displayed it, as a memorial to the long-ago former owner of our house and this former studio.

But now, instead of hanging pride of place on the den wall, the flat, felt hat was perched on my head. I'd tied its faded ribbons under my chin, and was staring at myself in the old, rust-spotted, silver-framed mirror (another looky-likey archaeological find in my den), wondering if I looked anything like Elize Grainger... Er, when she was *thirteen*, not when she was a hundred, when the local paper came around here to photograph her in our/her garden. (That newspaper cutting was pinned on my noticeboard, waiting to be framed, same as Nana Jones and Grandad Eddie's photo. When I'd looked earlier in the week, the only frames Woolies had were pink and inflatable, which didn't seem too appropriate.)

"D'you think it suits me?" I turned and asked Peaches.

He'd followed me out here to the den after breakfast, watched me text TJ (I hadn't had a reply yet), and kept a sleepy eye on me as I packed my pad and coloured chalk pencils into my rucksack so Mum and Dad believed my cover story.

"Well?" I quizzed him, seeing a whole lot of no response to my question.

And then I heard a rumble of a snore start up.

"Yeah, you're right. I look like a bit of a dork."

Maybe old-time floppy felt hats suited Elize Grainger (and they did – I'd seen her family portrait in Portbay Museum, dated 1840), but with *my* sproingy curls, I just looked like I was balancing a soggy, circular piece of cardboard on the top of my head. But I soon stopped wincing at my reflection when the sumo-wrestling poltergeists started up with today's bonkers noises. . .

"EEEEE-aaaaahhh-ooohhh-*yoooooooo*! EEEEE-aaaaahhh-ooohhh-*yoooooooo*!"

Hey, that was whole *new* noise coming from the house over the lane! Over the last few days, we'd had a "CLANK! CLANK! CLANK! *ScreeeeeeecchhhHHHH!*", then a "THUDDY-THUDDY-THUD-THUD, *booooooinnnggg!*", then a "Take that! And THAT!", a "Rat-a-tat-TAT!", followed by "Thumpety-thumpety-*thump*. . .", and then the very similar "*Thumpetty-thumpetty-thumpetty-DOOF*". And who could forget "*La, la,*

 99

la, la, la-LA-LAHHHHHH", and "CLANG!-*boiiinng*- CLANG!-*boiiinng*- CLANG!-*boiiinng*"? Not to mention last night's "*THUD-a-dud-a-dud-a-dud, THUD-a-dud-a-dud-a-dud, THUD-a-dud-a-dud-a-dud*".

That was it – I grabbed the chair by the desk and was determined to drag it to the bottom of the garden, clamber on it and get a good look at what was going on, binoculars or no binoculars. And then a completely different sort of noise made me stop in my tracks: a sudden crash, followed by a loud half-shout, half-groan.

"Andy?" I heard my mum call out from somewhere in the house.

Hearing the brittle edge of alarm in her voice, I dropped the chair with a clatter and went running through the garden and indoors.

"What's happened?" I panted, after taking the stairs two at a time.

Mum was crouched on the bathroom floor, next to my confused-looking dad, who was rubbing a hand through his tousled blond hair.

"He was taking the old cistern off the wall," Mum began to explain, pointing to an empty space up near the ceiling and then down to the cistern, which was lying sideways in the bath. "But it suddenly gave way when he was unscrewing it."

"Luckily, I managed to break its fall with my head!" said Dad, trying to be funny, even though his face was a strangely grey shade of white.

"Help me get him up, Stella," said Mum, putting one of Dad's arms around her shoulders. I was only too glad to help – maybe I'd been feeling a little bit resentful of Dad (and Mum) over the TJ thing, but now that he was hurt, I had a bad case of worried butterflies crashing about in my tummy.

"Is he going to be all right?" I asked Mum, as we began leading him down the stairs.

"Course I'm all right, Louise!" Dad interrupted brightly.

I'd have been more reassured if Dad hadn't a) been swaying, and b) called me by my mum's name. . .

"I think he might have a bit of concussion," said Mum (aka Louise), ignoring Dad altogether, "so I'm going to take him to the hospital – it'll be quicker if I just drive him straight there, rather than call an ambulance. Can you look after the twins?"

"Of course!"

As I spoke, I glanced down at the foot of the stairs and saw one skinny little boy and one pudgy one staring up at us with quivering lips.

One minute later, as I helped lower Dad into the passenger seat of the car, the twins were in full, megawatt wailing mode.

"WAAAAAAAAAAAAAAAAAAAAAH!"

"DAAAAAADDDDDD*DDEEEEEEEEE*!"

"Thanks, Stella," said Mum, smiling fleetingly, as she tried to disentangle Jake's arms from around her leg and get into the driver's side.

"No problem," I told her, holding on to Jamie, but leaning away from him so that his piercing howls stood less chance of puncturing my eardrum.

"Oh, and Stella. . ."

That was Dad, leaning over Mum in the driver's seat and grinning up at me.

"I know I'm supposed to be concussed, but are you *really* wearing a Victorian bonnet, or am I just seeing things?"

"You're seeing things," Mum told him, while throwing me a wink and starting up the engine.

As they drove off, I didn't know whether to laugh, cry or join in the wailing. . .

CHAPTER 11

A sudden case of deaf, dumb and blindness

"*RING-A-DING-A-DOSIES*!" the twins yelped happily in unison, with matching chocolatey smiles.

It had taken a whole hour, but my brothers had *finally* stopped wailing.

Even after Mum phoned to say that Dad was fine (there was just a bit of a dent in his head and he was probably going to have a headache the size of Finland), Jake and Jamie *still* wouldn't calm down. But then I guess when you're not quite two and a half, it's hard to be rational and grown-up. In fact, the only way I'd got the boys to cheer up was to put my hat back on and pull stupid faces. Once that got their attention, I told them we were going somewhere *really* special (Mum had asked me to take them round to the Little Acorns workshop thing, 'cause her and Dad wouldn't get back in time). I explained that in this really special place, they could play with *lots* of other children, and have the *best* fun. They'd both stared at me, not looking exactly convinced, till I added, "And we'll buy Chocolate Buttons from the shop on the way."

So, now, I was shoving the double buggy and sticky boys along the High Street, aiming for the community centre – down near the harbour – where my brothers could run riot and I could sit back, relax, read my magazine, and maybe try texting TJ again.

Or. . .

Or maybe I wouldn't have to *bother* texting him, 'cause (speak of the devil) there he was! Across the road, over the top of the jam of day-tripping cars headed for the beach, I could see a bunch of taller lads and one floppy-haired smaller one. So TJ was hanging out with Sam and that lot today; I s'pose maybe *that* was why he hadn't got back to my message.

"TJ!" I called out, waving my hand more madly than I meant to in my excitement.

Four (tall) heads turned towards me, while a (shorter) one dropped down to stare at the ground.

"Hey, TJ!" I tried again.

Er. . .

Hadn't TJ heard me above the growl of the

104

traffic? Well, his mates certainly had, and were now grinning over like I was a penguin who'd just done a bellyflop in the zoo pool. Even Bob the blimmin' dog had heard me: through a momentary gap in the traffic, I could see him gazing across, recognizing the sound of my voice and giving me a friendly, answering "Wuff!" *Unlike* his master, Bob *hadn't* been struck down by a severe and unexpected case of deaf, dumb and blindness.

"STELLLAAAA! Don' stop!" Jake roared, wondering why we weren't going anywhere any more.

Ignoring my little brother's demand, I tried yelling again.

"TJ!"

Nothing. If anything, he dropped his head even lower to the ground.

I gripped tightly on to the buggy handle, stunned, as TJ and his mates (and Bob) turned into the alley where The Vault was. One of the lads – couldn't tell 'em apart yet – turned and gave me a sarky little wave before they disappeared.

I still didn't move, though I could feel my cheeks flooding pink. I had just been blanked, by my supposed friend. What in Bob's name was all *that* about?

And then it dawned on me . . . pants!

Had TJ told that bunch of boys about what had happened with Jake and my knickers?

Urgh, the *shame*. . .

For the first time in days, I suddenly felt like the old, stammering, *wincingly* shy Stella again – the part of me that I didn't so much love as loathe. And for the first time in days, I felt myself pining for Frankie. *Frankie* wouldn't have let those lads have the last laugh (or the last wave) over my stupid polka-dot pants. She'd have done or shouted something that would have burst their smug bubble, just like she had last Friday, when she stood up in the Shingles café and blew those boys a big, fat, fake kiss. They hadn't known where to look, mainly 'cause they probably hadn't come across a girl who was just as swaggering and full-on as *they* were.

That made my mind up; as soon as I got Jake and Jamie to playgroup, I was going to text Frankie. But first I'd have to get my legs to move . . . once they'd stopped being paralysed with mortification.

"Toffee?"

Candyfloss, apple pie, lemon cheesecake . . . just for a second, the faintest syrupy-sweet waft tickled under my nose, so that even before I turned to see who was offering me a sweet, I knew it was Mrs Sticky Toffee herself.

"Um, no. . ." I shook my head miserably at the rustly plastic bag being held out towards me.

The old lady, in her shimmery-green raincoat and ridiculous hat, tut-tutted at me kindly.

"Don't be silly – it's only a little bit of toffee!" Mrs S-T smiled at me from under her pink netting meringue. "Sugar gets a bad press and that's for sure, but it has its good points. Gives you a little energy boost, so they say, *and* it's good for shock."

Shock. . .

How could Mrs S-T have known I'd just had a shock?

But she doesn't, I told myself off. *She's just waffling, and you're making out it means something. . .*

"Thank you," I mumbled, giving in and taking a wrapped sweet out of the bag.

"Not seen you for a while, dear! Settling in to the town all right?" Mrs S-T asked, while stuffing the toffees back in her tiny, shiny cream handbag and rifling around for something else.

"Um, yes, thanks," I told her, realizing as I spoke that not only hadn't I seen Mrs S-T for a while, but I hadn't wandered over to Sugar Bay – to Joseph's

107

house – for ages either. Somewhere inside, I felt a ping of pining, a bit like I'd had when I thought of Frankie, my faraway best friend. . .

"Now for these little brothers of yours," muttered Mrs S-T, pulling out a puffy, pillow-sized bag of marshmallows, that seemed *way* too big to have come out of such a tiny handbag.

"Ta!" grinned Jake.

"'Ank yooo!" gurgled Jamie.

As the boys gently reached a hand each in to take a marshmallow, LOADS of muddled thoughts swirled through my befuddled brain:

1) I'd never seen Jake and Jamie so polite and well-behaved. Yeah, maybe when they were *asleep* they were totally good, but *never* when they were awake.

2) How did Mrs S-T *know* they were my brothers?

3) Well, it was a pretty straightforward guess, I suppose. I mean, who *else* would they have been? A couple of kids I'd stolen while their mum was choosing sausages at the butcher's shop we'd just passed?

4) Frankie . . . thinking about her all of a sudden reminded me of that one weird moment in the den yesterday, when TJ had said, "Yeah, I know," when I pointed out her photo on the

corkboard. Still didn't know what (if anything) to make of that. I should ask him. . .

5) . . . if I ever spoke to him again, of course. I mean, why had he acted like I was poo on his shoe just now, when yesterday, he'd really, *really* felt like someone who could be . . . well, *someone* to me? *Was* it because he'd told those lads about my knickers being on show, and was too shamed to look me in the eye 'cause of that?

6) Had my parents been right to be wary of him, 'cause of him hanging out with Sam's gang? Had I got it 99% wrong, and he was 1% an idiot after all?

7) Would my legs *ever* recover any feeling, or was I destined to be stranded here with the boys and the buggy, like some mad human statue on Portbay High Street? (Hey, maybe if enough tourists threw money at me, I could collect the train fare back to London for a visit. A *long* visit, preferably. . .)

"Friends of yours?" asked Mrs S-T, a marshmallow lodged in her cheek, as she nodded in the direction of the lane, The Vault and the now-disappeared lads.

"No," I said, unwrapping the toffee I was holding and hoping it would take away the bitter taste of disappointment in my mouth.

"Nice bunch of lads . . . to their mothers if no one else," Mrs S-T surprised me by saying bluntly. "Though you can't go tarring everyone with the same brush, can you, dear? There's always a chance of one good apple being hidden away in a barrel of rotten ones."

In the couple of conversations I'd had with Mrs S-T since I'd come to Portbay, she'd managed pretty successfully to confuse and bamboozle me, and today's little chat was going to be no different, it seemed. I'd grown up with Aunt Esme's weird and wonderful home-made proverbs, but Mrs S-T's muddle of sayings made no sense at all.

Unless. . .

Unless in her own freaky way she was trying to hint that TJ might not be as bad as the other lads?

OK – now I just remembered the *other* problem with talking to Mrs S-T . . . she was loopy, and made *me* feel loopy. (It was catching.)

"Uh, I'd better go," I said, while giving my legs a quick, nearly invisible shake just to check they would work. "Got to take my brothers to playgroup. Thanks for the sweets . . . and, um, everything."

"Pleasure, dear!" Mrs Sticky Toffee called after

me, as I hurried off as fast as humanly possible while pushing a heavy buggy laden with little boys. "And just remember, you can't judge a book by its cover!"

She might as well have said "you can't judge a fish by its bicycle" for all that meant to me.

"Lady NICE lady!" said Jake, tilting his head back and gazing at me with an upside-down grin.

"Lady MAD lady!" I muttered back to him.

Then I bit hard on my toffee, and imagined it was TJ's head. . .

Chapter 12

The end of the line. . . (Boo-hoo)

"'Nother 'mallow!" shouted Jake.

"'YESSS! 'Nother 'mallow, Stewwa!" Jamie chipped in.

Bleep!

Gee, *thanks*, fate. Thanks for arranging a text from my best friends to arrive *just* when I'm feeling particularly friendless. I mean, I *really* wanted to be reminded of all the fun they were having together in London, when the only company I had here at the back of beyond were two small boys who were demanding more *marshmallows*, for goodness' sake.

Start end-of-the-line project 2day! On northern line now! Will tell u more l8r. . . Par x

OK, here's what that was all about: you really *yearn* for school holidays, right? And then – kind of *tragically* – they can turn out to be mind-blowingly boring. Well, it was like that back at Easter, for me and my mates; we all overdosed on mooching around the shops and hanging out at Hampstead Heath (where we kept getting rained on).

So we got talking about what sort of stuff we could do in the summer holidays. Everyone came up with ideas, but not all of us were dead keen on putting together a hip-hop dance group (thanks, Neisha!), or working our way through every martial arts movie in the video shop ("You have *got* to be joking!" Frankie had sniggered at Lauren). Then Parminder came up with the end-of-the-line project. She pulled out the foldaway tube map of London in her Filofax and pointed at the coloured spaghetti of the criss-crossing tube lines. "See? They all end *some*where. But where? What do all these places *look* like?" Me and Frankie and the others bent over and began reading out random names, like Stanmore (sounded posh and sensible) and Morden (sounded depressing) and Cockfosters (sounded rude) and wondered what would be there when you got out of the tube and gawped around.

Anyway, the idea just seemed to wriggle its way into all our brains: this summer, we'd hop on a different tube every day, and see what there was to see at the end of the line.

But for me, the project had one small flaw; my

parents decided to move. So today, while my mates were trundling on a tube train to High Barnet, I was trying to ram a double buggy through the stubborn doors of a community centre in downtown Portbay. (How thrilling . . . *not*.)

Yep, you've probably spotted that I was feeling just a tiny – OK, *huge* – bit sorry for myself. But there was *one* good thing about that; caught up in self-pity, along with the burning anger and humiliation I felt when I thought about TJ blanking me, I'd managed to stomp my way boldly into a noisy room crammed with strangers (of the mum and children variety), and had sat down and freed my brothers from their buggy straps before I even *remembered* to be nervous.

In fact, it was only when I heard a familiar tippety-tappiting coming towards me that I snapped out of my thundercloud of a bad mood and properly took notice of what was going on around me.

"Hello, Jake! Hello, Jamie! Hurrah! You've come to play!"

"Ellie!" I said in surprise, taken aback at seeing this tap-dancing, smiley bundle of five-year-old blondeness right in front of me.

For a split second, my heart went squish, as I

panicked that TJ was here too. But then the little bit of common sense I had took over and told me that *couldn't* be right; he'd probably still be hanging out in The Vault right now, trying to impress his stupid mates or stupid Sigh or Si or whatever the boy in the shop was called. I could picture TJ now, trying to look cool, nodding his head in time to some track booming out of the speakers, even though none of his so-called friends would probably be able to *see* him over the top of the CD racks. . .

"Hello, Stella! Do you like my tap shoes?" Ellie asked blithely, holding up one foot right under my nose so I could get a really good look at her shiny, black, bar-strap shoes and the frilly white lace of her ankle socks. "I have to take them off in a minute, because Mummy says it's a drama workshop and you can't wear tap shoes in a drama workshop, but that's not fair, is it?"

"Er, no," I said, with a shake of my head, even though I wasn't very sure if I thought that or not, since I couldn't really figure out what kind of drama workshop you could *have* with such tiny kids like there were here today.

Which reminded me, I really should (urgh!) find the teacher and tell her that Jake and Jamie were here for the first time.

"Um, Ellie – which one is the teacher?" I asked her, feeling my mouth already going dry with nerves as I scanned the women in the room.

"My mummy, course!" Ellie giggled. "Mummy! Come and say hello to TJ's friend!"

A woman standing chatting only a little way away turned and came towards us. So *this* was TJ's mum, this person dressed head-to-toe in primary colours? She looked like she'd matched her red baggy trousers, blue trainers, green T-shirt and the yellow scarf (bundled in her wavy fair hair) to my brothers' Duplo bricks. How had I managed to miss her when I first came in? She was totally out of place in this big, drab, grey hall; she should have been on the set of a CBeebies show, singing about being a bee or something.

"Oh, how lovely! Stella, is it?" she beamed at me, her head of curls bouncing as she tilted her head enquiringly at me. "I'm Caroline O'Connell. And do these two little rascals belong to you?"

The twins were playing up as usual: Jamie had hold of Ellie's foot and was trying to wrestle her tap shoe off while Jake was pulling off his sandals and chucking them without looking to see who they might hit.

"Y-y-yes," I replied, steaming fast into the rest of the sentence, hoping that if I hurried, the stammer wouldn't get a chance to happen again. "They're my brothers. The chubby one's Jake and the skinny one's Jamie."

O'Connell . . . so it's TJ and Ellie O'Connell? I repeated in my head, processing the information. Not that I needed to know TJ's last name, not if we weren't going to be friends any more.

"Well, I'm sure the boys will have a *marvellous* time here, and my little sweet pea Electra will help settle them in, won't you darling?"

Electra!

"Yes, Mummy!" Ellie/Electra giggled, as she hopped around, trying to stop Jamie from making her lose her balance.

"Now if you'll excuse me, Stella, I'd better get the class started!" Mrs O'Connell smiled my way as she began to walk off. "And now that you and my little pumpkin Titus are friends, I'm sure we'll be seeing a lot more of each other!"

I didn't know which to be more horrified about: the fact that Mrs O'Connell had referred to TJ as her "little pumpkin", or the fact that she was to blame for naming him *Titus*. . .

It's just . . . *Electra* and *Titus*! Weren't they like ancient Roman or Greek names or something? Why had TJ's mum (and Dad) thought ancient Roman names went with an Irish *last* name? And what on earth did the "J" stand for? "Jupiter"? "Jehovah"? "*Jam*"? No *wonder* TJ liked to be called TJ. And no wonder he got a bit funny that first day we hung out and I tried to fool around and guess his name.

I mean, imagine being short for your age, *teased* about it, lumbered with a terrible name *and* having a mum that dressed like the sort of kids' telly presenter who sings "The Wheels On The Bus Go Round And Round" while doing *all* the actions?

Y'know, for just a second there, I felt a sort of flurry of sympathy for TJ. And *then* I remembered that he'd made a total prat of me (and possibly my pants) in public and decided he deserved everything he *got*. . .

"OK, little ones!" Mrs O'Connell called out, clapping her hands. "We're going to have *such* fun today! And let's start by warming up our voices by shouting a big 'hello'!"

As thirtyish small children shrieked, shouted, roared and bellowed a deafening chorus of raggedy "HELLLLLLLOOOOOOO!"'s in the hall, I winced, and wished I was far, far away – preferably on the Northern Line to High Barnet, North London. . .

ChapteR 13

Revenge is sweet-ish

OK, stupid question, but can a house be your friend?

Let me put that another way; I had this sudden feeling that I really, *really* wanted to go over to Sugar Bay, to walk in the silent, deserted, echoing rooms of Joseph's house. It's just that I'd gone from resenting Dad, to stressing over him getting hit by a toilet; then there was the humiliation of being blanked by "Titus", and the sheer trauma of sitting through the Little Acorns shout-a-thon workshop. I was emotionally drained and it was only quarter to one this Friday lunchtime. And strangely, the only place that seemed calm and safe and *right* right now was the old broken-down derelict mansion that Elize Grainger had once called home. The only thing stopping me from rushing over there straight away was a matching pair of tired small boys who needed taking home for refuelling.

"Hey, Mum – it's Stella," I said into the mobile I'd tucked under my chin. (You can't push a double buggy with one hand; it'd be like trying to kick a fridge-freezer up a hill, believe me.)

"Hi, Stella! Where are you?"

"Just walking along the prom," I told her, watching seagulls swirl and white-edged waves tiptoe up the sands on the beach below. "So, how's Dad?"

"He's fine. When we got home, he was determined to get back in the bathroom to finish it off, but I've told him to lie on the sofa and relax, or I'm divorcing him."

"Oh, yeah? Well, that's OK, only what are we supposed to do if we need to use the loo, since half of it's lying broken in the bath?"

There was a couple of seconds of muffled silence, then Mum's whispered voice crackled on the line again.

"Sorry, had to get out of Dad's hearing range. He doesn't know it yet, but I called the emergency plumber to come round and fix it."

Poor Dad. Practically every DIY effort he had made so far had to be properly fixed or finished off by a professional someone-or-other. But when it came to our family's bladders versus Dad's feelings . . . well, there was no contest really.

"Anyway, how was the Little Acorns thing?" Mum asked, daring to raise her voice again.

"Awful," I moaned.

"Awful how?"

Where did I start? Awful as in awfully boring, awfully pointless, awfully embarrassing, or plain awfully *awful*.

"The teacher made all the kids pretend to be really corny stuff," I told Mum.

"Like?"

"Like . . . like they had to act out being little acorns."

"Which was what, exactly?" Mum asked, sounding like she was smiling.

"They had to curl up really small, and stay really still for ages."

"And Jake and Jamie managed to stay still for *how* long?"

"About five seconds."

I grinned to myself, remembering the frown on Mrs O'Connell's face when Jake reached his five-second patience threshold, uncurled himself and started singing "*HUMPTEEE-DUMPTEEEE SA' ON A WAAAAA'!*" at the top of his voice.

"Oh, dear. . ." Mum sighed, though I knew from the hint of the giggle in her voice that she found it pretty funny. "But listen, tell me more when you get home – I think I hear your dad getting up and moving about. I'd better check he isn't trying to grab a power tool or something."

I'd no sooner said bye and ended the call when a familiar *bleep!* bleeped. Stopping the buggy for a second – right beside the ornate drinking fountain – I checked my incoming text.

High Barnet – boooorrrring. Dumping end-of-line project! Par x

Parminder couldn't have sent me a better message at a better time – at least I wasn't missing out on maximum fun with my old friends *after* all. OK, so now instead of feeling 100% lonely, I only felt about 75% lonely, which wasn't much difference, but as Frankie's mum used to say, "If you can't be glad for small things, then you're a very sad kind of person." And I was *determined* not to be a sad kind of person.

"Doggy drink!" Jake suddenly giggled.

I was just about to text Parminder a quick reply, but instead I glanced around to see what my brother was on about. He was pointing to the bottom of the water fountain, where – sure enough – some kindly Victorian architect had made a marble trough of water at doggy-drinking height. I hadn't noticed that before, when I stood here to meet TJ earlier in the week. I hadn't noticed the inscription on the water fountain either.

"'For the refreshment of the townspeople and animals of Portbay, presented by Miss Elize Grainger, 1880'," I mumbled in surprise.

I was also surprised to see a familiar hairy head appear as I read that out.

"Bob dog!" Jamie gurgled, as Bob (the dog), stopped lapping thirstily and smiled up at us.

Uh-oh; if Bob was here, that meant. . .

Before I'd even got to the end of that thought, four mean 'n' moody tall boys and one dumb 'n' dopey short one ambled up the steps from the beach, hands shoved in pockets, shoulders hunched up.

As four sets of eyes fixed sneerily on me, I fumbled my phone back into my pocket and got ready to push the buggy off at high speed the second I heard anyone shout *anything* to do with underwear. . .

And then something made me hesitate; a jumble of somethings about finding one good apple amongst the rotten ones, and not judging a book by its cover. My thoughts might not have made much sense (much like Mrs Sticky Toffee in general), but I knew I had to give TJ one more chance to make it right, to show that blanking me

123

earlier had been just an accident, or maybe just a stupid mistake, and nothing to do with knickers.

And so I fixed my eyes on TJ . . . and got my answer immediately. This time, there was *no* excuse. I wasn't half hidden or drowned out by holidaymakers driving by in their Volvos. I was *right* here in front of him, with two small boys yelling his dog's name loudly, and his dog nuzzling my hand for a pat. But *still* TJ dropped his gaze to the paving stones and pretended that I was as invisible as a cold germ.

Bubbles of anger and humiliation began rumbling through my chest again, when – out of the corner of my eye – I noticed a huge seagull flap itself down on to the top of the fountain, and stare ominously down at the group of lads; or, more likely, at one person in *particular* in that group of lads. And that suddenly put an idea in my head, an idea about getting my *own* back. . . Oh, yeah, the old, shy Stella just wanted to run away fast, and ignore the fact that TJ was doing a very good job of ignoring *me*. But the new, improved, *braver* Stella had something *else* in mind. . .

"Hi, Titus!" I said very loudly, very brightly, staring *very* hard at TJ.

And with that, I held my head high, gave Bob

a quick farewell scratch on the head, and strode off with the twins and the buggy, feeling almost giddy with surprise at my own courage.

"*Titus?* TJ, your name's *Titus?*"

Just like I'd known they would, Sam's gang immediately began hooting and roaring with laughter. Yep, with those two little words, I'd got my revenge. I felt *well* happy.

Until I glanced over my shoulder and saw the sad, crumpled face gazing at me from the midst of the hooting, horrible lads. . .

CHAPTER 14

Sorry, with strawberries on top

"What a *prat*! Don't you *dare* go feeling sorry for him, Stella!"

It was Saturday morning and Mum had gone to the beach with my brothers, and taken Dad with them, since he was still banned from doing DIY or anything else that required a brain for a few days. Downstairs, the proper plumber (who was getting very familiar with our house, since he'd already had to fix pipes Dad had broken) was clattering about, finishing the job he'd started yesterday, when Mum had called him out.

And me? Well, I'd told my parents that I wanted to stay home and have a yak with Frankie, which is exactly what I was doing now, spilling all about TJ, since there was no point in keeping it to myself any more – not now I'd found out that my instincts were 99% wrong and he was truly a 1% idiot.

"Well, it wasn't so much that I felt *sorry* for

him exactly," I tried to backtrack. "It was just that when those lads started teasing him about his name, this look came over his face that just made me feel a bit, I dunno, sort of. . ."

". . .sorry for him!" Frankie finished my sentence for me. "Look, he's mates with a bunch of mutt-heads, so you're better off without him!"

Frankie was right, which is why I was glad I'd phoned her and poured out all of yesterday afternoon's humiliation, but she still didn't seem to *get* the fact that I was kind of disappointed to see my first potential friend in Portbay slip-slide away. . .

"Uh-oh . . . listen, Stell – I didn't realize the time. I promised my gran I'd be round to hers at ten to take her out shopping, and it's nearly ten now. Can I call you back later?"

"Yeah, course," I told her, as I scratched Peaches' purrily vibrating head.

As we said our hurried goodbyes, a sudden loud *loudness* from outside threatened to drown us both out.

Bedooooiiiinnnnnnggg-TWANG!
Bedooooiiiinnnnnnggg-TWANG!
Bedooooiiiinnnnnnggg-TWANG!
"Huz*aaaahhhHHH*!"

"What are they *doing* over there?" I wondered

out loud for the trillionth time, as I clicked the end-call button and chucked the phone on the bed.

"Prrrp!" said Peaches in reply (ish), as he stretched himself into a luxurious arch on the bed, and casually clawed the phone closer to him, as if it were a catnip mouse.

"I *might* be able to see something if they hadn't got their curtains closed," I muttered, peering out into the sunshiney brightness and seeing the darkened windows of the house opposite.

Peaches yawned and began to do the reverse of his big stretch (i.e. he more or less ignored me).

"Hey, *I've* got an idea!" I said, turning around and clocking Peaches now tucking his legs up underneath himself like a furry picnic table. "Maybe I could attach a tiny camera to your collar, and you could sneak your way into that house to see what's going on?"

There were times when I convinced myself that Peaches was psychic, but it didn't seem like he had much of a sense of humour. Or maybe he just thought *my* sense of humour was a bit lame. Whatever, he went right on purrily blanking me and began staring purrily at my phone, two millimetres from his neat little nose, his green eyes practically *crossing* it was so close.

Meanwhile, I went back to staring out the window, straining my ears for more weird, inexplicable noises, and tried *not* to think that only two days ago, I thought that maybe me and TJ could have fun trying to suss out the source of the noises together. . .

When my mobile suddenly started trilling, I jumped, but Peaches didn't seem to. When I whipped my head round and hurried over to the bed, I saw that his once-crossed eyes were nearly closed and his whiskered snout was almost mimicking a Cheshire Cat grin. For some reason, it reminded me of my mate Eleni, when she'd go guessing the end of movies when we were only halfway through watching, and then give us all this *told*-you-so smug smile when the lights went up.

"Hello?" I answered, frowning a little since I hadn't recognized the number flashing up on the phone panel.

"Stella?"

Now *there* was a voice I hadn't expected to hear, even if *Peaches* had. . .

Her name was Amber; it said so on a rectangular badge pinned to her dress. I'd seen her a couple of times before when I'd been here in the Shingles café, but I'd never known what she was called.

"You want something?"

The grumpy, red-haired teenage girl was hovering over me, a pad in her hand. Not just her cheeks but her whole *face* was flushed red, like she was really angry with me for daring to be here and bother her with my order. Or maybe it was just that she realized that it was one of *my* little brothers who'd tripped her up while she was carrying a full tray of dirty dishes last time we were in here.

Still, annoying as that must have been for Amber, it was hardly as embarrassing as what happened to *me* last time I sat at this very same table with my family and Frankie. I mean, it was *my* head that Amber spilt a plate of cold pasta over, after all. . .

"Er, strawberry milkshake," I croaked out, trying to keep my eyes from wandering over the terrible black cotton dress and white apron the tall, skinny girl was wearing. She was obviously job-sharing that old-fashioned get-up with another waitress; one who was a lot *shorter* and *squatter*, by the looks of it.

I wished TJ would hurry up . . . even though the café was packed, I felt kind of awkward and conspicuous sitting here in the window seat, like a bug-eyed goldfish in a pet shop window. It

130

didn't help that I felt I was being stared at from a table at the back by Rachel and Brooke and whatever the rest of the café crew were called. (Help. . .)

But never mind them; the other reason I wished TJ would hurry up was that I was *dying* to hear what he had to say . . . I mean, *apart* from the garbled snatch of conversation we'd had on the phone half an hour ago, when he'd said stuff like "sorry about yesterday" and "can we meet in the café?" and "I just want to explain and everything".

So what *was* TJ's explanation "and everything" for ignoring me (twice)? Well, I was still waiting to find out but then I *had* got here a few minutes early, I realized, checking the time on my mobile on the table in front of me.

Desperate for something to do so that I didn't look to the *entire* clientele of the café (especially Rachel and co) like I'd been stood up, I thought about texting Frankie – but felt too stupidly fidgety to think of a message and ditched that idea for now. Tapping my nails on the pink plastic coating of my phone, I gazed around, letting my eyes settle on the front page of an open newspaper some old man was holding up and flicking through at a nearby table.

131

Vandals Strike Again! screamed the inky black headlines of the *Portbay Journal. Teen gang thought to be responsible for—*

"Hi!" said TJ, sliding into the seat opposite. "Didn't know if you'd come!"

He was hunched down low in the chair, wearing his "I'm With Stupid!" T-shirt, a nervous smile on his face. He suddenly reminded me of Dexter, Lauren's kid sister's hamster, who looked cute but concerned at all times.

"I didn't know if *you'd* come!" I told TJ, realizing too late that I was smiling. Drat – I'd planned to act all aloof till he explained himself properly. "Er . . . who're you waving at?"

TJ was looking somewhere over my shoulder, wiggling his fingers half-heartedly at someone-or-other.

"Just Rachel and that lot," said TJ, sounding pretty unenthusiastic.

"Thought you said you didn't think much of them?" I said, remembering a snatch of conversation we'd had that first, excellent day we'd spent together, crazy golfing and talking rubbish.

"Yep, I think they're a bunch of stuck-up moos, but they're waving at me, and I'm not up for falling out with people unless I really have to."

"Oh," I mumbled uselessly, guessing that he included me in that, or we wouldn't be here.

"Anyway," said TJ, stopping with the finger-wiggling and flashing me a nervous-ish smile, "this is the same seat you were sitting in the very first time I saw you!" he blurted out.

"The first time. . .?" I frowned. "But the first time we met was on Monday, down on the beach!"

"Um, *yeah* . . . that was when we *met*," TJ shrugged. "But it wasn't the first time I *saw* you. The first time I saw you was last Friday night, when you were in here with your mum and dad and brothers and stuff. When your mate Frankie blew that kiss over to us, when we were sitting up at the back of the caff. . ."

Blam.

Cue surprise, shock, horror, etc.

"Um . . . you mean you were with Sam and those lads that time?" I gasped in surprise.

But then (doh!) it sort of made sense; that's why TJ had recognized Frankie's picture when I showed it to him in the den, wasn't it? And another thing; that evening, same as now, there was a big gormless Alsatian tied up outside Shingles. 'Cause last Friday, hadn't Dad taken Jake out to pat the dog, while Mum had gone to the loo with Jamie? That's when me and Frankie

133

were left alone, and Frankie had cheekily blown the kiss to the gawping boys. . .

Seeing me glance his way just now, Bob put a hopeful paw up on the glass at the other side of the plate-glass window.

"But why didn't you tell me before?" I turned to ask TJ, while reaching my hand out to "touch" Bob's paw from *my* side of the glass.

"Well, you'd already talked about the lads, when we were walking to the crazy golf on Wednesday, and you said how they'd laughed at you and taken the mick out of you the first weekend you'd moved here," TJ shrugged. "So I didn't think you'd exactly be too *chuffed* if you knew *I* was there with them last week. Specially not 'cause of what happened, when Amber spilt all that stuff all over you. . ."

As I quietly cringed, I guess I understood why TJ had stayed schtum about that, even when we were getting on well.

OK, so that was fair enough . . . but then *why* didn't he seem to care about my feelings *yesterday*, when he completely blanked me?

"When you phoned this morning you said sorry. . ." I mumbled, dragging the conversation around to the *real* reason we were here.

"Yeah . . . yeah, I mean sorry for not talking to

you when I saw you yesterday. It's just that Sam and them are kind of *funny* about girls. I mean, they *fancy* some of them – like Rachel and *her* lot," TJ explained, nodding his head in the direction of the cliquey girls posing at a table at the back of the café. "But they don't think it's cool to be *mates* with a girl."

"So, *that's* why you ignored me?"

"Uh-huh," said TJ, wincing and looking pretty ashamed of himself, I was glad to see. "I know it's dumb, but they've only just sort of accepted me, and I didn't want to, y'know, go and mess things up."

Oh, yes, yes, *yes* . . . none of this had ANYTHING to do with my knickers, by the sound of it. (Phewwwwww. . .)

But I still needed to ask TJ a straight-out question.

"So does that mean we're friends – or not?"

"Course we are!" said TJ, looking sheepish again, and starting to agitatedly spin a stray teaspoon around on the table with his finger.

I was about to ask him how it was going to work exactly; if that meant he was going to act like he knew I *existed* next time we bumped into each other when he was with Sam and the others. But a strawberry milkshake and a sour face interrupted us.

135

"There you go," Amber announced flatly, thudding the tall glass down so hard in front of me that my phone rattled on the formica table. "What *d'you* want?"

"Nah, nothing," said TJ, glancing up at her and shaking his head.

Amber seemed to flush redder, furious at TJ taking up valuable bum space without buying anything, and stomped off with a clatter of her chunky black shoes.

"Can't stay," he suddenly told me, ignoring Amber's glaring huff. "Mum's got a class to teach this afternoon, so I've got to get back to look after Ellie."

At the mention of Ellie's name, a little ripple of guilt wibbled its way up my spine. Maybe *I* should take a turn apologizing.

"Er, I'm sorry I called you Titus in front of Sam and everyone. I just wanted to embarrass you, 'cause you'd embarrassed *me*. . ."

"That's OK. I guess it makes us sort of even," TJ shrugged across the table. "So Mum told you, huh? She said she met you at that kid thing she runs."

"Yeah," I nodded. "Pretty fancy names she landed on you and your sister!"

"They were names from plays she was in at

drama school," TJ explained, wrinkling his nose in what looked like disgust.

"Um . . . can I ask you something?" I ventured, wondering if I was about to be *way* too cheeky. "If Titus is the 'T', what's the 'J' stand for?"

"'J'," he repeated, idly spinning the teaspoon around on the table.

"Yeah, the 'J'," I nodded.

"No – the 'J' is just for 'J'. That was my dad's idea. He said that if me and Ellie didn't like our first names, then we should get to choose our second names ourselves, but he thought it would be fun to give us just an initial to start us off."

Wow, that was the first time TJ had ever mentioned his dad.

"So," I said slowly, "*you're* Titus J O'Connell. . ."

". . .and Ellie's Electra Z O'Connell," TJ finished my question off for me. And then disaster struck.

"Oh– oh, no! *Sorry*, Stell. . .!"

Y'know, when it came to the Shingles café, I think I was *jinxed*. After all, *last* weekend, I'd ended up with carbonara dribbling down my neck; today, TJ had made a grab for his spinning spoon and managed to spill the whole of my strawberry milkshake on to my lap.

"Oh, God . . . *here*! Take this!" TJ muttered,

137

looking as red-faced as grumpy Amber the waitress, while he yanked handful after handful of paper towels out of the serviette dispenser and chucked them at me.

"It's OK, TJ," I tried to tell him, even if it didn't really feel OK to have sticky pink milk seeping through my T-shirt and denim miniskirt.

"Look, you better go to the loo and wash some of that stuff off," TJ bumbled. "Maybe they've got one of those blow-dryer things. . ."

"Yeah, I will," I nodded, getting to my feet and clutching bundles of serviettes over the worst of the stains. "Back in a sec. . .!"

No surprises, but it took more than a sec. And no surprises, but I heard a couple of bitchy, witchy comments from a certain table at the back when I was on my way to the loos ("What a *state*!" "Yeah, *again*! Ha, ha, ha!")

Whatever . . . a few minutes later, as I stood holding my soaking (but cleanish) T-shirt under the hand-dryer in the ladies' loos, I vowed a couple of things. First, never to speak to Rachel and her stupid, snippy girlfriends, whether they were in my year at school or not; and second, *never* to moan again about my name. It's just that I *used* to feel self-conscious about being called after something showy like a star when I was so shy, but compared to the real, full names poor TJ and Ellie had been lumbered with, Stella was plain and simple and just about *perfect*.

Checking in the toilet mirror that I was still dampish, but at least not *pink* any more, I headed back out to the café (blanking my eyes and ears to the table closest to the loos) . . . only to find a totally strange family sitting at the window seat, and no Bob outside the window staring in either.

"Thought you'd sneaked out without paying," said the waitress called Amber, gruffly shoving a bill in my hand.

"Um . . . do you know where my friend went to?" I asked her.

"Dunno. His mates came. He left with them," she said bluntly, obviously desperate just to get me to pay and go, so she could get on with her job of being rude to other customers.

Titus J O'Connell, I thought to myself as I stepped out of the bustling café and into the blazing sunshine, *what ARE you playing at. . .?*

CHAPTER 15

The secret of the sweet-talking trick. . .

I'd tried to get hold of Frankie first, to tell her what had happened, but she must've still been at her gran's or something. Whatever, her mobile was switched off and there was just the answering machine on at her house.

"So there was no sign of PJ when you came out of the café?"

Auntie V had always been rotten at remembering the names of my London friends, and it looked like she was going to be exactly the same with any *new* friends I made here in Portbay. Not that I was entirely sure at the moment about whether I could count on TJ as a friend or *not*. . .

"No. I mean, TJ *did* say he couldn't stay long 'cause he had to babysit Ellie. But it's just the fact that he didn't wait to say bye, and just went off when Sam and the others turned up."

"Stella, darling, you've already told me the

poor boy has a chip on his shoulder about his height. If his mother mollycoddles him and his parents give him a name that's too impossibly over the top to live up to, no *wonder* he's rebelling a bit and hanging out with the bad boys!"

"But it's not fair, Auntie V!" I protested. "He's supposed to be my friend too!"

"I didn't say it was *fair*, Stella my little star, I'm just saying it's totally understandable!"

When I'd got back home, the plumber had finished clanking about for the day, and my mum and dad *still* weren't back from the beach with the boys. As I had the place to myself, I'd plonked down on the sofa with the house phone and called the *one* person I thought might understand what I was going through. But since Frankie wasn't around, I was now wondering if the *other* person I thought might understand really understood at *all*; I mean, it almost sounded as if Auntie V had decided that TJ was better off hanging out with Sam and the other lads instead of *me*.

Hadn't she?

"Listen, I could be wrong, but PJ sounds like a bit of a sweetie."

OK, so maybe I'd got that wrong. And at those

very words of Auntie V's, Peaches – presently curled up fatly on my lap – began purring so hard I practically felt myself vibrating.

"Well, sometimes I think he *is*, and sometimes I think he *isn't*," I replied.

Just like sometimes I felt sorry for TJ and sometimes I didn't.

"You know, Stella; I somehow think he'll come to realize that those boys aren't *true* friends – they're only using him for their own entertainment; having a laugh at his expense, by the sound of it. You'd be a *much* better friend to him."

"I know – but what can I do?"

"Enough of *my* gut feeling, Stella, darling – what's yours? Do *you* think PJ's worth one, last chance?"

It was like the volume and vibrate buttons had been turned up to "10" somewhere on Peaches' furry body – his manic purring was getting more insistent by the second.

"Um, yes . . . I guess," I told her.

Peaches blinked loving eyes at me. The big, fat, catty weirdo.

"Well, in *that* case, you're going to have to sweet-talk him, darling."

"I have to *what*-y?" I double-checked.

"Sweet-talk him! I just mean, be your usual funny, lovely self, try to think of great things to do together, and whatever you do, *don't* slag off his friends, or that'll make him defensive about them. It's *then* that he'll realize that you're *much* more gorgeous a person to hang around with than those horrible, sarky boys."

"Are you *sure* that'll work?" I asked dubiously.

"It's a trick that's worked for me *many* a time. And it certainly worked with your dad, when we were teenagers."

"What – that time you were telling me about, when he got into trouble, with – with the paintballing thing?"

"Oh, yes. Have you talked to him about that yet?"

"No. . ."

"Well, I'm not going to spoil that story for you – I'll let him tell you himself. God, I'd *love* to see the reaction on his face when you ask him!"

"Auntie V!" I groaned. "You can't *not* tell me now!"

"Yes I can!" she replied breezily. "But I *will* tell you that he was hanging out with a few *morons* at the time, and I told him, actually I *yelled* at him that he was being the biggest moron of the lot for being friends with them. Course that got me nowhere, so I decided to change my plan."

"What did you do?" I asked, moving slightly to adjust the weight of Peaches, since the feeling was starting to go in my legs.

"Well, like I say, I tried the sweet-talking technique. I decided to be *extra* nice to your dad, with sugar on top. It confused him – for a while – but sure enough he came round, and started moaning to me about his mates and their exploits. I just tried to be sympathetic, and eventually it dawned on him that they truly were berks and I was *completely* brilliant!"

The way Auntie V came out with that, I was giggling so much that I didn't clock the sound of the front door opening.

"Hey, is that laughing I can hear? What a nice sound to come home to!" said Dad, his beaming face appearing in the living-room doorway. "It must be that mad Frankie you're talking to!"

"Is that your DIY-disaster, former teen terror of a father?" Auntie V whispered in my ear.

"Yes, it's Dad, and no, Dad, it's not Frankie, it's Auntie V!" I replied, answering both their questions at the same time.

"Great! Let me have a word with my favourite sister then!"

Dad strode across the room enthusiastically, holding out his hand towards the phone, leaving Mum out in the hall to deal with the twins.

"S'pose I'd better have a word with that doughball of a brother of mine!" Auntie V muttered in my ear, making me giggle again. "Anyway, bye for now, Stella, darling – and good luck with the sweet-talking!"

As I handed the phone over to Dad and gently poured Peaches on to the sofa, I found myself excited, i.e. kind of quiveringly hopeful that her advice would work.

"Hey, I think these two brought half the beach home with them!" Mum laughed, as I went through to the hall and found her unstrapping the damp, happy, sandy twins from the buggy.

I smiled; half at the blissfully messy boys, and half at the knowledge that later, after lunch, I'd go out to the den and text TJ. I wouldn't mention the fact that he ran out on me at the café – I'd just suggest that we meet up tomorrow or sometime to do something fun, like hang out at Sugar Bay. . .

"Ooh, that's *lovely*!" Mum suddenly announced, pausing with a *Finding Nemo* bucket and spade set and a nappy-bag in her hand. "What *is* that smell? It's like peaches and cream, almost!"

I glanced down as Peaches curled his way around my bare ankles, gazing up at me with his adoring green almond eyes, and knew instantly that he *totally* approved of my plan. . .

The amazing, disappearing mobile

I was feeling sick.

I was feeling *so* sick that I hadn't been able to face the full-on Sunday morning mega fry-up breakfast that Dad had put in front of me this Sunday morning.

"Not hungry, Stella?" Mum said, frowning at me across the table, noticing that I was doing a great job of swirling beans in an interesting pattern around my sausages and not much else.

"*Ish*," I answered her, forcing myself to nibble the end of a sausage so Mum didn't think I was going anorexic on her or something.

"Are you *sure* you're OK, Stell?" Mum frowned some more, studying my face for signs of impending illness.

"I'm fine!" I lied, feeling really, horribly *sick*.

"Don't fuss, Louise!" Dad said good-naturedly, as he reached over for another newspaper from the bundle he'd brought back from the shop this morning. "If Stella isn't hungry, then she's just not hungry. And it means *all* the more for me!"

Flicking a newspaper upright with one hand, he expertly nicked the other *un*nibbled sausage that was on my plate with the other.

After that, thankfully, Mum *did* get off my back, giving up her line of questioning with a roll of her eyes at Dad.

"So . . . what're the local headlines then?" she asked him instead, getting back to eating her own breakfast, while keeping a wary eye on the boys in their high chairs. (They were eating nicely and quietly now, but knowing them, a food fight could break out at *any* minute, with lumps of soggy Weetabix and eggy toast being chucked at anything that did or didn't move.)

"The local headlines . . . well, let's see," said Dad jovially, while scanning the paper.

"Let me guess. . ." said Mum, as she put a hand out to stop Jake spooning bits of breakfast on to the floor. "*Man Grows Giant Turnip*? Or how about *Nothing Happened In Portbay This Week Shocker!*"

"Hmm, not quite!" Dad replied, all of a sudden furrowing his eyebrows together. "Listen to this; *Vandals Strike Again! Teen gang thought to be*

responsible for spate of smashed phone boxes and bus shelters around town."

"Oh!" Mum gasped, looking a bit flustered.

I didn't really listen while Dad read out the whole story to Mum; I was too busy feeling sick. Sick because my mobile was gone. Gone, as in missing . . . lost . . . stolen. . .? I didn't know which. I'd only realized that I didn't *have* it any more when I went to text TJ after I'd spoken to Auntie V yesterday afternoon on the house phone.

I'd checked in my room, in the den, around the house, in case I'd put it down somewhere without thinking. Then I checked under cushions on the sofa, *under* the sofa, and down the *sides* of the sofa, in case it had slipped out of my back pocket when I was chatting to Auntie V on the regular phone. I noseyed in trainers, in the washing machine and even down the new loo, in case one of the boys had been playing hide-the-mobile when no one was looking.

When I'd searched everywhere and couldn't find it, I'd pretended to Mum and Dad that I wanted to go down to the High Street to see if any other shops sold frames for Nana Jones and Grandad Eddie's photo – and instead, hurried straight to the Shingles café to ask if I'd left my mobile there and if anyone had handed it in. "No," red-faced Amber had said bluntly, as she carried a teetering tray of ice-cream sundaes to a table of OAPs. That was the end of that – it must have dropped out of my pocket when I'd been walking home at lunchtime, maybe.

And so the rest of yesterday, and all this morning, I'd felt sick. The thing was, it wasn't just *losing* my phone that was making me feel sick, it was the whole keeping-secrets thing that was making me feel yucksville too. Y'see, I hadn't got round to telling Mum and Dad about losing my phone yet – not 'cause they'd flip *out* at me or anything – but because the first thing they'd say would be "When do you last remember seeing it?". And the answer to that was at the table in the window of the Shingles café – with TJ. Spot the secret? I hadn't told them I'd seen him, just 'cause I thought they had that silly downer on him. If I went and told them now, they'd probably blame TJ for making me turn all secretive on them. God, they might even go putting two and two together and come up with some totally mad idea that TJ had something to do with my phone going missing. . .!

Stella – this is stupid! I suddenly thought frantically to myself. *Mum and Dad wouldn't*

necessarily think bad stuff like that! And maybe
they don't have that much of a downer on TJ at all –
maybe you just overreacted the other day when they
were talking about him. . .

I was just about to offload and spill the news about my mobile when Mum got in there first by gazing up from the *Portbay Journal* and asking me something.

"Stella – that gang that you said your friend TJ was hanging about with. . . Um, you don't think maybe *they're*—"

"Mum!" I gasped, a sudden rage coming over me before she'd even finished her sentence. "You're *always* telling me not to jump to conclusions about people! And those boys that TJ knows aren't exactly going to be the *only* teenage boys in the whole of Portbay!"

"You're right, Stella," said Dad, looking a bit shamefaced. "We shouldn't jump to conclusions, it's just that your mum and I thought that when we left London we'd be moving away from any potential trouble like this. . ."

"I'm not hungry – I'm going to go and e-mail my friends," I muttered, getting up from the table and not responding directly to Dad's semi-apology.

It felt kind of mad that I'd just stood up for

four boys that I didn't even know properly but knew enough not to *like*, but I hated hearing my parents act all bigoted in that way. Not to mention hypocritical. . .

If I could bear to go back in the kitchen right now, I'd ask Dad about what he got up to as a teenager – that whole paintballing thing that happened – see how guilty he feels then! I thought darkly (even though I didn't have a clue what I was on about), as I sat down in front of the computer and waited for it to boot up.

"*Hi Stella!*" I read, as Frankie's message pinged on-screen. "*Sorry I had to dash off to Gran's yesterday, but you know what a state she gets in if me or Mum are ever late round to hers (thinks we've been run over by a double-decker bus or something). So what's new with you?*"

I stared at the screen and wondered where to start. I *wanted* to tell Frankie about meeting up in the café with TJ after I spoke to her, but since she already thought he was a loser, I had a feeling she'd freak out at me if I told her a) that I'd seen him at *all*, and b) that he did a disappearing act on me. And if I told her *that* stuff, then I should also tell her that I was thinking of giving him (yet) another chance – and somehow I didn't think that Frankie would be too wild about Auntie V's

152

sweet-talking trick. ("*Sweet*-talk him? Tell him where to get off, more like!")

I stared at the screen some more and tried to figure out how I could put it across without Frankie telling me I was insane. But I didn't get very far, mainly 'cause the doorbell rang and – out of habit – I started running to answer it, till I remembered we *weren't* in Kentish Town, where my mates popped round all the time, and so whoever was at the door probably wasn't calling for *me*.

Wrong.

"Stella! Visitors for you!" Dad's voice drifted through to the tiny office I was hunched up in.

I think it was the scrabble of claws on bare floorboards that gave it away before I got through to the hall and saw my dad standing chatting brightly and towering over TJ.

"Hi, Stella!" said Ellie brightly, before her brother got a word in edgeways. "Can I go see Jake and Jamie, please?"

"Um, sure – they're in the kitchen with Mum."

And in a blur of pastels she was off.

"Hey, really, *really* great dog, this – eh, Stella?" Dad grinned at me, as he ruffled a grateful Bob's head. "And I was just saying to TJ that it's *excellent* to meet him at last!"

TJ was smiling at me too, but there was a slight panic in his eyes – I could tell he was totally confused by how over-the-top my dad's welcome was. But *I* knew what Dad was up to; making up to me *big*-time, to prove he *wasn't* making presumptions about TJ and his other mates. I kind of appreciated the effort, but it was pretty cringeworthy to witness. . .

"And hey –" Dad suddenly added, pointing at the "I'm With Stupid!" logo across TJ's skinny chest – "cool T-shirt, dude!"

"Dude"? My dad just said "Dude"? *Omigod*. . .

And it didn't stop there; Mum and Dad both flurried embarrassingly around TJ for so long – offering him sausages, bacon sarnies, orange juice, carrot cake, spare keys to the *house* practically – that it took about ten minutes for the both of us to get away from them and escape out into the garden (with Bob).

"They're all right, your mum and dad," said TJ as we ambled towards the den.

(*You wouldn't be saying that if you'd heard what they were talking about five minutes ago*, I thought.)

"Yeah, they're OK," I shrugged, as I tugged at the stiff hook that kept the door safely shut against inquisitive toddlers.

"Is it all right to leave Ellie with them? She's not going to bug them, is she?" he asked, chucking a thumb over his shoulder in the direction of the kitchen, where we could hear Ellie belting out some old Kylie song, pausing for intermittent tapping breaks.

"Hey, if she's keeping the twins occupied, my parents will love her for *ever*."

Out of the corner of my eye, I spotted TJ grinning at that remark of mine, and suddenly realized how pleased I was to see him.

"Glad you came round!" I told him, pushing the door open.

(Notice something? I could have opened with "What happened to you yesterday?", but I didn't – Operation Sweet-Talking TJ started *here*, whatever Frankie might have thought of it. . .)

"Yeah, well, I just . . . *whatever*," he said vaguely, looking momentarily shy or something as he followed me into the den.

"Hey, check this out!" I smiled, pulling my latest photo-strip of the girls off the corkboard.

As I pointed out Eleni and Parminder and Neisha and Lauren to him, my brain was working overtime, wondering what sort of sweet-talking I could do to win him round. I should have asked Auntie V for some examples. . .

"Hey, *she's* pretty cute!" said TJ, his index finger right next to Neisha's face.

"Well, she'd think *you* were pretty cute too! She likes indie boys!"

"Yeah?" said TJ, shuffling awkwardly, but looking kind of chuffed, all the same.

Brilliant – that was a successful bit of sweet-talking I'd done there, even if it wasn't exactly true. I mean, Neisha liked her boys hip-hop flavoured. Dunno *what* I'd do if she came to visit sometime and they met up, but I'd have to worry about that later (or get TJ to swap his grunge T-shirts for some serious street style).

Be-*doinnnnnngggggg*, be-*doinnnnnnnggggg*, be-*doinnnnnnggggg* – "WHEEEEEEEEEEEE!" – *thud*.

"What was that?" asked TJ, his eyes wide.

"Our spooky neighbours, up to their spooky stuff again," I explained.

"Wanna take a look?"

"Sure!" I said, grabbing the chair by the desk.

TJ beat me to the bottom of the garden, of course, mainly 'cause I was humfing the chair with me. And Bob beat me too, since he bounced fearlessly through the thigh-high weeds, wild flowers and nettles, instead of taking wary baby steps like me.

156

"Wait!" I called out, as TJ started scrambling up the bricks. "You can stand on the chair!"

"S'OK! I'm good at climbing!" he said, already pulling himself up on to the top of the wall.

"What can you see?" I asked him, trying to take a step up on to the wooden chair but realizing my denim mini was too tight for such a big step up.

"Not much. . ."

TJ had one jeaned leg dangling on our side of the wall, and the other dangling on the lane side.

". . .they've got their curtains closed."

"That's the same as last time!" I sighed, giving up on wriggling my skirt up a bit and clambering on the chair if there was nothing to see.

"But hold on," said TJ, suddenly darting his head around like an inquisitive chicken as he peered towards the house over the lane. "The curtains aren't *totally* closed. I think I can just see something moving. . . *Urgh!*"

Something moved all right – TJ scrambling at hyper-speed off the wall, and tumbling into a sniggering heap on a clump of dandelions and dusty earth.

"What happened? What did you see?" I urged him, kneeling down beside him.

It was almost infuriating; he was laughing so much he could hardly get his breath, let alone speak. It wasn't just me who was getting wound up; Bob was frantically pacing backwards and forwards around his master, snuffling at him like he was worried he'd broken something or gone mad. The only one who was calm was Peaches, who'd appeared out of nowhere (no surprise there) and jumped up on the den chair. He was staring coolly at TJ, like the headteacher waiting for the hyperactive kid to calm down before giving him a telling-off.

"Someone – someone –" TJ started to hiccup out, sounding a bit like me at my stammering worst.

"Someone *what*?" I demanded.

"Someone started opening the curtains – they nearly caught me!"

I was shocked, absolutely shocked.

"Stella?" said TJ, concern in his slightly breathless voice. "Did you hear what I said?"

Yes, of *course* I'd heard what he'd said, but I was too shocked to care about stupid, weird neighbours and their stupid mystery noises when I'd seen what I'd just seen.

TJ hadn't registered Bob rummaging his snout in his master's jeans' pocket just now. But as he followed my stare, he soon saw what was wrong.

"Oh, God. No, it's OK, Stella – I can explain!"

But exactly *how* TJ was going to explain away what Bob had innocently grabbed out of his pocket, I had *no* idea.

"Good dog," I said to Bob, gently taking my mobile phone from between his teeth. . .

The dare, and big, old, dumb me. . .

Outside in the sunlight, butterflies hovered prettily, bees buzzed busily, and dragonflies soared and dived over our tangled garden like it was a prickly kind of paradise.

Inside, I sat hunched over my desk in the den, trailing my finger over the carving I'd done in the windowsill last weekend: *Stella + Frankie, M8s 4eva, 2004.*

Frankie and me, mates for ever . . . and there was me and TJ, whose friendship had lasted for a whole four *days.*

Hey, who'd have guessed that sweet-talking TJ would stop before it even started? But then, who'd have guessed I had such crappy judgement when it came to people? Or that I'd end up picking a lying, cheating thief for a potential new friend?

Still, TJ had certainly tried his best to sweet-talk *me.*

"I was going to give it back to you! That's why I came today! I didn't *want* to nick it!" he'd tried to explain, stumbling up out of the dandelions and dust, as I'd stared blindly at the dog-drool-covered mobile in my hands. "It's just . . . well, I *knew* it was all wrong, but then when your mobile rang and it was one of your mates, it felt *really* wrong."

Now it made sense – the end of Frankie's e-mail, I mean. TJ was the mystery boy who'd answered her call yesterday.

"They said I had to do it!" TJ blundered on with his excuses, while I was too dumbstruck to say anything out loud about anything. "They said that they'd tell *everyone* at school what my name really was, unless I did a dare!"

Bob – picking up on the fact that something was wrong, even if he couldn't figure out what that might be – dropped his hairy head on to my lap and gazed up at me with soulful brown eyes.

"And I said, fine, I'd do the dare – but then Aiden said the dare was to nick something off *you*!"

I didn't care about the dare; I just cared that I'd stuck up for TJ in front of my parents and Auntie V, and been so dumb as to give him a big, fat, sweet-talking second chance.

"Ben said it didn't matter what it was I nicked off you, but then Sam said it couldn't be something lame like a hairslide or whatever, it *had* to be something important. And then when I met up with you in the Shingle, I thought, I just can't *do* it. But after I spilt your milkshake and you went to the loo, the lads all turned up at the window, and Marcus was tapping on the glass and pointing at your mobile. You'd just left it sitting there on the table. And – and –"

Er, was TJ making out that it was almost my *own* fault that he'd stolen my phone? No way – he'd stolen it because his other "friends" egged him on. His other "friends", who mattered more to him than *me*. . .

"Hey, guys!" Dad had suddenly called out from the open kitchen doorway. "We're just going to have some ice-cream. You want some?"

I said nothing, mainly because my vocal chords were temporarily paralysed with shock. TJ stared beseechingly at me for a second, but seeing that I wasn't too likely to say anything any time soon, he did the talking for me.

"No thanks, Mr Stansfield!" TJ'd called back, brushing the dust off his jeans. "Me and Ellie have to get home now!"

And with that – and a whispered "Sorry,

Stella!" – TJ clambered across the garden towards the house, calling Bob after him.

And that's when I'd come in here to the den, to lick my wounds and straighten my head out.

"What am I going to do, Peaches?" I softly asked the purring furball sprawled out across half the desk. "I know *you're* my friend, but who else have I got here?"

Slowly, Peaches elegantly clambered to his feet, and after a wide catty yawn, he shook himself, like a dog caught out in the rain. Only, instead of sprinkles of water, Peaches sent a fine shower of glinting, golden sand shimmering out of his scruffy ginger fur.

And then I knew.

"You all right in here?" Mum asked, peeking around the door of the den.

"Yeah," I nodded, even managing a smile. "I was just thinking about going out for a walk."

It was quite possibly bordering on the insane, but my best friends in this town so far were a fat cat, an old lady, a house and a couple of ghosts I hadn't even *seen*. And I'd been neglecting one of them in particular lately; I hadn't been to Sugar Bay and the old mansion there in *way* too long. . .

The frazzle marble

My Granny Stansfield (my alive-and-cuddly-and-living-in-Norfolk grandmother), has these blue-as-the-sea beads that she brought back from Portugal once as a souvenir. "They're worry beads!" she explained to me when I was little, and loved to hold the cool, smooth string of stones in my pudgy little hands. "If you're worried, you're meant to run the beads through your fingers – and doing that over and over again will calm you down and help you think more clearly."

Well, right now I wasn't so much worried as frazzled. And I might not have had a set of worry beads, but I *did* have a marble. Did that count?

Walking down the windy lane from my house, I'd come across the green marble tucked in the pocket of my shorts. It was the one I'd caught Peaches playing with on my bedroom floor a few

164

days ago. I'd meant to stick it in the den, in the bowl that held shells and stuff, but I'd forgotten all about it.

Anyway, as I was stomping in the direction of Sugar Bay, my feet took an unexpected detour – and I blame the marble for that. I'd been rolling it around in my fingers, trying to defrazzle my brain from tangled thoughts of TJ, when I found myself . . . lost.

I hadn't come across this little street of higgledy-piggledy houses before, but my pink flowery flip-flops seemed to think that this was a perfect short cut to the path that would take me up over the headland to the Seaview caravan park, and the shiny, sandy bay just beyond it.

It wasn't till I caught a glimpse of the street name that it dawned on me exactly where I was.

"Pottery Lane. . ." I murmured, staring at the street sign on the corner of the old building, and hoisting the slippery nylon rucksack further up on to my back.

Pottery Lane, I repeated in the privacy of my head. *This is where he told me he lived. I even remember the number; "Thirteen, same as my age, this year anyway!" he'd joked. . .*

All that random stuff that TJ had spoken about last Wednesday, on the way to the crazy golf;

165

whether I wanted it to or not, some of it had seeped into a filing tray in my head.

At the thought of suddenly running into him, I got a bad case of the frazzles again and started spinning the marble madly in my fingers.

TJ wouldn't have had to do the dare, if you hadn't told those lads his name in the first place. . . I thought bleakly, feeling a twinge of guilt.

Flippety-flop, flippety-flop, flippety-flop. . .

My flowery flip-flops were at it again, leading the way till I found myself in front of a big shiny red door, with a less-than-shiny brass number "13" screwed dead centre on it. To the side, three plastic bells were stacked one on top of the other on the doorframe, with scribbled or printed names underneath each one.

"'Holman'," I murmured reading the first one. "'Brown', 'O'Connell'."

Before I could chicken out, I pressed on the third option.

"Ah-woo-ooo-ooo, oh yeahhh!"

Er . . . I was pretty sure that was Mariah Carey warbling away. Since I hadn't expected an American singing diva to answer TJ's intercom, I was just about to let go of the buzzer and run away as fast as my flip-flops would let me, when I heard *another* voice.

"Hello?" said someone who didn't sound very old.

"Ellie?" I asked, hearing an insistent barking in the background – as well as Mariah – and knowing that I had definitely got the right flat.

"Who's that?"

"It's . . . it's Stella," I spoke into the impersonal plastic box.

"Stella!" the little girl's gleeful voice warbled down. "Come up!"

And so half a minute later – just slightly out of breath – I found myself on the third floor of the building, being let into a flat that smelled of flowers and sherbet, perfume and incense, shower gel and *dog*.

"Hello, Stella!" said Ellie, looking extra small and dainty as she held open the heavy, old-fashioned door.

"Wuff!" barked Bob, tappity-tapping his claws with excitement on the varnished floorboards, as if he was doing an impression of Ellie at her tap-dancing best.

"Ah, hello . . . Stella, isn't it?" smiled Mrs O'Connell, coming out of another room in a rush of steam, wearing a piled-up white towel on her head and a deep orange kaftan-type thing. "I *thought* I heard the doorbell when I was getting

167

out of the shower just now and wondered who on *earth* Electra was letting in. So how are you? And how are those adorable brothers of yours?"

Maybe Mrs O'Connell wasn't a very good actress, because when she smiled and called Jake and Jamie "adorable" you could tell she didn't mean it. At all.

"They're fine," I mumbled, finding myself following her into the living room, while Ellie slipped a tiny hand into mine.

Thankfully, Mrs O'Connell went to turn the CD player down. I know some people adore Mariah Carey, but I always think her voice is like someone just *shouting* in tune.

"So what brings you around, Stella? Got a message from Titus, that little rascal of mine?" asked Mrs O'Connell, talking to me via her reflection in an ornate mirror above the mantelpiece, as she loosened the towel and freed her damp wavy hair over her shoulders. Right beside her was a huge glass vase of giant tiger lilies. I could just imagine Mrs O'Connell casually tearing one off to tuck behind her ear.

"Er . . . no. I . . . I sort of hoped he'd be here," I tried to explain, glancing around the huge room, which seemed awash with yet more vases of flowers, competing with vivid flowering potted plants for exposure. And every corner of the room seemed to radiate colour, with jewel-coloured satiny throws and cushions draped over two fat sofas and several saggy armchairs. I'd never seen such a hippie, girlie room and I'd never seen so much stuff crammed on someone's walls. I mean, back in London Eleni's living-room walls were decorated with the most amazing gold icons of the Virgin Mary and all sorts, but Mrs O'Connell's room was totally different. You could hardly see the fuchsia-pink walls for bookshelves and CD racks and Indian wall hangings and Victorian-ish posters advertising old-fashioned potions and pills. And any spare bits of wall seemed to be made up of a patchwork of blown-up photos of Mrs O'Connell when she was younger. They were "stills"; the sort of publicity photos from plays and musicals that Auntie V had up on *her* office walls. And then there was this one shot of a huge, tall, tanned guy with a chest the size of Ireland and a tiny kid on his shoulders.

"That's my daddy!" Ellie explained, spotting what had caught my eye. "That's TJ up there! I wasn't even not nearly born!"

How weird . . . now I looked at it, it was like someone had superimposed TJ's face on to Arnold Schwarzenegger's body.

"Oh, that," said Mrs O'Connell flatly. "Yes, that's my ex-husband. That was taken in America, when he got his first break over there."

"He's an actor too?" I asked warily, sensing that Mrs O'Connell was about as fond of TJ and Ellie's dad as an attack of killer bees.

"Was. He's now a stuntman in Hollywood," she said with a sneer. "Doing fantastically well, apparently, though he doesn't bother to get in touch with us that often to tell us himself. I'd take that photo down, only Titus won't let me."

Squish. . .

That was the sound of my heart softening for poor TJ. Apart from everything *else* that could give him a chip on his shoulder, how could TJ a) live up to an Action Man dad who paid him no attention, and b) feel comfy living in Hippie Barbie's house? Him and Bob must stick out here like a pair of old socks in a basket of kittens. . .

"Oh, dear – what *is* Titus like!" sighed Mrs O'Connell, turning away from the subject of TJ's dad and checking the time on the clock on the wall. "He is *such* a naughty little pumpkin. He *knows* I've this rehearsal for the Portbay Gala show this afternoon, and that I need him to look after Ellie. And what does he do? Comes home and leaves this smelly dog of his, then goes out again without a *word* of explanation, slamming the door behind him! *And* he's not answering his mobile. Where on earth can he be?"

I knew *exactly* where he'd be . . . hanging out somewhere with a bunch of lads he didn't even *like*, all because he thought he'd driven me away as a friend.

I *wished* I could tell him he hadn't. . .

A crashing tinkle or a tinkling crash?

After I escaped from the Hippie Barbie flat, I tried to phone TJ – but like his mum said, his mobile was switched off. Walking along I scanned the skies, hoping to spot a lurking seagull that might lead me to him, but with no luck.

And so I'd decided to go back to Plan A, and head over to Sugar Bay, at the same time letting the sea breezes blow thoughts of TJ out of my still-frazzled head (I hoped).

Now here I was, little me on a huge chunk of headland.

Stretched out endlessly in front of the headland was a vast expanse of sea, out over the horizon towards infinity. (Er . . . though I guess *technically*, over the horizon was *France*, but that's a bit less poetic than "infinity", isn't it?)

Behind me lay a bunch of ugly old caravans. (And there wasn't *anything* very poetic to say about Seaview Holiday Homes, especially since they spoiled a very picturesque spot.)

I was doing my best to ignore the caravans – and getting my breath back after the climb up the path to get here – by stopping and soaking up the sea view through the viewfinder of Mum's camera, which I'd shoved in my rucksack when I left the house earlier. Sweeping to the left, I could make out the packed beach at Portbay. Sweeping to the right, the deserted golden sands of Sugar Bay curled around in a perfect, unspoiled crescent. And if I turned right just a teeny bit more, I'd be able to see –

EEK! A *face*! A huge, distorted face *leering* right into the lens!

"Hello, dear!"

As soon as I heard that – and sniffed the scent of something sweet – I dropped the camera down, and found my view of Joseph's house blocked by a small, smiley, ordinary (ish) old lady.

"Uh, hello!" I nodded, wondering if Mrs Sticky Toffee had any other clothes apart from her apple-green raincoat and her pink netting nest of a hat.

"I've only seen you doodling with your pencils before," she smiled, her cheeks dusty with a layer of face powder that old ladies seem to have to wear by law. "Didn't know you were a bit of a snapper too!"

I wasn't *really* a snapper too. It was running my fingers along the "*Stella + Frankie, m8s 4eva*" carving in the windowsill of the den that had put the idea in my mind. I'd decided that I *had* to get myself to that upstairs room in Joseph's house and take a photo of the original carving that'd inspired me: "*Elize and Joseph, friends for eternity*". . .

Then something suddenly fluttered into my mind; I still hadn't been able to point out Mrs Sticky Toffee to my parents . . . maybe I could show them a photo of her instead? At the same time, I could get Dad to scan it into the computer for me, and zap it off to Frankie etc. And (of course) I should take a photo of Peaches, and my den, and the view out of my window and stuff too. . . Frankie had seen all that, but my other mates hadn't.

"Can I take your picture?" I asked Mrs S-T, holding the camera up.

"Oh, no, dear!" she shook her hand, making the small cream handbag dance around in the crook of her elbow. "I'm far too old and ugly. I'd just crack the lens!"

I was sort of disappointed by her answer, but it seemed rude to insist. And I was too shy to tell her that she wasn't ugly at all – she was lovely, like . . . like an icing-sugar-coated meringue or something.

"Toffee?" offered Mrs S-T, like a consolation prize for refusing my request.

As we unwrapped our sweets and let the strangely sweet, salty, buttery tastes tingle over our tongues, me and Mrs S-T stood in silence, staring out at the view.

"Kissed and made up with your friend yet?"

I nearly choked on my toffee.

"S'cuse me?"

"The boy on the other side of the High Street when I met you. That nice one. Not very tall, but a big heart."

"Um . . . not really," I mumbled, hoping she wouldn't ask me any more, since the whole TJ situation was way too complicated to start explaining to a stranger. Even a friendly, toffee-sharing stranger.

Luckily, what I said seemed to be enough for her, and we went back to staring out at the dancing white-tipped waves again.

"You know something?" Mrs S-T started up again, after a whole few moments' silence. "She'd have *hated* to see the tin cans here. She had *totally* different plans, you know. . ."

I *didn't* know, but that was because, just like always, I wasn't really sure what Mrs S-T was on about.

"Sorry?" I squeaked.

"The caravans – they wouldn't be here if Miss Grainger had had her way. Oh, no," Mrs S-T shook her head, as if what she just said was as plain as day, instead of as clear as mud.

"But . . . but they must have set up this caravan park *long* after she died," I frowned, doing some maths in my head. The newspaper cutting I had of her was celebrating her 100th birthday in 1930 – and the caravan park might have looked a bit tatty, but it must only have been here since the 1960s or 70s.

"Oh, yes . . . but Miss Grainger *loved* the view from this spot, when there was nothing much up here apart from grass and rocks," Mrs S-T smiled. "She always hoped to one day build holiday homes and an arts centre here, specially for underprivileged children – children from the slums of London. She needed to find a buyer for the old house down in Sugar Bay to afford to do that, but – of course – it never *did* sell."

I blinked and looked out at the view again, and thought about the fact that there were no actual *proper* slums in London any more, but there were still plenty of families struggling for money, and kids who never got to see the seaside, never mind go on holiday. It would have been brilliant to think of a place here that they could come to over the years. . .

"So, you're off down to Joseph's house now, are you, dear?" Mrs S-T burst into my thoughts. "Lovely day for a picnic there."

"I wasn't *planning* on having a picnic," I frowned at her, trying frantically to remember if I'd actually *mentioned* that Joseph's house was where I was heading.

"Oh, well you must take *these*, then, dear!" Mrs S-T insisted, pulling a clear, plastic bag of mini fairy cakes out of her mini-sized handbag.

"But, I – I couldn't," I bumbled, staring down at the grass in total shyness. "I mean, it's really *nice* of you . . . but I couldn't just take them. I mean. . ."

I fluttered my eyes upwards, hoping Mrs S-T could understand my nervous attempts at politeness, but. . .

But there was no one – apart from a lone, swirling gull in the sky – *anywhere* on the headland with me.

So what could I do except pick the bag of fairy cakes up off the grass and carry on down towards Sugar Bay. . .?

*

177

It was a crashing tinkle.

Then again, maybe it was more of a tinkling crash.

Whichever, it made my heart take a downward, bellyflopping *dive*. . .

A few minutes ago, I'd been walking down the hill towards Joseph's house, feeling strangely light-headed. Part of it was to do with Mrs S-T trundling off at surprisingly high speed for someone so old, and then there was also the fact that I'd been passing the time on the downhill path by gawping at the sun through my frazzle-marble. The warped rainbow of shades refracted through it was prettier than any of the colours of chalks in my art box in the den. I'd still been silently "wow!"ing about that when I stopped dead outside the railings to the garden of Joseph's house, halted by the newly erected sign that Portbay council had thoughtfully placed there.

"*Condemned Building,*" it reminded me bluntly, "*. . . demolition due 30 August . . . proposed new development by Seaview Holiday Homes. . .*"

I mean, yeah – what this bay needs is fewer historic mansions and more stupid caravans, I'd thought to myself, right before I heard the crashing tinkle/tinkling crash, and the roar of raucous laughter that followed it.

Hurriedly shoving the marble back in my pocket, I dipped through the space in the metal railing where a post had rusted to dust and crouched my way through the undergrowth of the former garden, towards the nearest open window.

"Hey, nice shot, Aiden!" someone was bellowing. "Your turn, Ben!"

"No problem!" a voice called out, followed by another shattering smash of glass and a growl of approval.

As I crept closer to the open window of the ballroom, I stretched one hand behind me and held on to my rucksack – it was probably just me being paranoid, but the rustle of the packet of fairy cakes I'd stuffed inside seemed deafening.

"Sam! Sam! Sam! Sam!" came a rhythmic clapping of hands and a call of voices next.

At the sound of another smash, a bellow of voices shouted, "*Yessss!*"

"C'mon, *Titus*! Your turn!"

"Yeah, *Titus*! *Do* it!"

As I stared upwards at the brick windowsill, my heart was doing a tap-dance in clogs across my chest, but I *had* to find out what was going on.

"No *way*!" I heard TJ's voice yell, as I willed myself to do a Peaches and leapt up to grab on to

179

the sill, my flip-flops softly and silently scrabbling for a hold on the wall.

"You've *got* to do it. He's *got* to do it, right, Sam?" I heard a mean, whiny voice say, just as I managed to lever my elbows to take my weight and get a look inside.

And then the swaying, dancing twinkles of light made me realize what was happening: the only grand thing left in Joseph's house – the great, ornate, crystal chandelier hanging from the ceiling – was being used as target practice by Sam's gang. . .

"Forget it! I already *said* I didn't want to do it!" TJ barked, chucking aside the stone or pebble being held out to him.

"Look, just chuck the sodding rock, *right*?" a menacing voice ordered.

I saw TJ stare out the lad who was speaking. And in that split second, I finally got my first proper look at the four tall boys. The one who'd just talked *had* to be Sam; he had the arrogant look of a ringleader, chin up, shark-eyed. The others were three nearly identical grinning hyenas, loving the wind-up, loving having someone to be mean to.

"Forget it," muttered TJ, stomping off towards the nearest window . . . and *me*!

"Hey, is that your *girl*friend, *Titus*?" snickered one of the hyenas, as my feet started scrabbling at the brickwork to keep my balance.

TJ stared my way, shocked to see my furl of curls and mess of freckles peering over the windowsill.

"*Aww*, going to dump us for your little *girl*friend, *Titus*?"

That was Sam's voice, his words drenched in sarcasm. Only I didn't get to *see* him say them, since flip-flops – as I found out at that precise second – aren't exactly reliable climbing equipment.

As I flumped into an ungainly pile on the ground, hunting around for the flip-flop that had pinged off, all I could hear was TJ saying one word: "Yes!" But in the couple of breathless seconds before he got the chance to scramble out of the window and bound down beside me, I noticed something odd. . .

It was yet *more* twinkling of light, coming from straight up above on the headland. At first I thought it was just the sun reflecting off one of the caravan windows, but then I realized it was a) moving, b) blue, and c) *flashing*. It wasn't until the police car came to a halt at the top of the path that I guessed what might be about to happen.

"Look, I'm sorry about that," TJ started twittering in explanation the millisecond his baseball boots hit the ground beside me. "I mean, I know you're not *really* my girlfriend, Stella, but I just *had* to get away from those dorks and—"

"Shhhhh! Stay *down*!" I ordered TJ, hauling on the edge of his T-shirt to get him to come down to my crouched level (which wasn't much of a drop for him, let's face it). "We've got to stay out of sight – follow me!"

"What are we doing?" asked TJ, copying my crawling routine through the matted under-growth of wild rose bushes and foxgloves. Somewhere above us, Sam's gang were still cracking up at TJ's expense before one of them realized they needed to get back to business and get on with destroying the chandelier.

Kerr-ASHHHH!

"*Yessssss!*"

"Look, the police are coming!" I looked back and told TJ urgently. "We've got to get away, so they don't think we've got anything to do with this!"

TJ's face went white, then red, then white again – but thankfully the shock made him speed up more than anything. And so a couple of swift-crawling minutes later, we were lying nearly flat in a dip in the sands not that far from the water's edge, sneaking a glance back the way we came, only to see three policeman cautiously creeping up to the house.

"How did they find out?" panted TJ.

"Dunno – someone up in the caravans must have spotted what was going on, or heard the noise, and called the police," I whispered.

"Listen, Stella . . . honest, I didn't know that's what Sam and them were coming here to do!" TJ looked at me earnestly. "I just thought we were going to hang out. *Then* they started boasting on about all the bus shelters they've done in, and started chucking rocks at that old, fancy light thing, and I thought, this is *bad* – I've got to get out of here!"

Ninety-nine per cent of me took one look at that pale, drawn face and knew he was telling the truth.

"They haven't sussed about the police being here yet," I said, shuffling around on to my side in the sand for a better look. "They're making too much noise!"

TJ nudged up on his elbow.

"Uh-oh. . ." he muttered, shrinking right back down just as quick.

"What is it?" I hissed.

"One of the policemen – I think he *saw* me.

183

What if he comes over? What if he checks us out? He could think we were with Sam and them, and trying to sneak away! What're we going to do?"

I couldn't believe what I came out with next. I could've believed *Frankie* saying it, maybe, but not *me*; not shy Stella Stansfield. I would have *sworn* on Peaches' life that I wouldn't have said something like that in a million, trillion years.

But I did.

"Kiss me."

"Huh?" TJ squawked, as loudly as the seagull that was now starting to swirl above our heads.

"Kiss me!" I repeated. "If the policeman looks over and sees a boyfriend and girlfriend snogging on the sand, he's not exactly going to suspect us of vandalism, is he?"

It only took TJ a panicked second to see sense, and another second to reach over and do what he was told.

I guess it's a strange way to have your first on-the-lips kiss – smooching a boy who's only a mate (and a much smaller mate; not that you could tell that lying side by side in the sand), with a seagull circling ominously above your head.

But as I had already started to suss out, I'd moved to a pretty strange kind of town. . .

ChapTeR 20

The shameful shame of the
you-know-what

I'd never been so glad to see a bird before.

Even if it was a big, bad-tempered one.

At least it meant that me and TJ had something to think – OK, make that *panic* – about, instead of . . . of you-know-what.

I mean, I couldn't speak for TJ, but personally, I was so totally embarrassed by the whole you-know-what, I felt pink all over. I could've sworn that even my *hair* follicles were blushing. . .

And on that fast, furious sprint away from Sugar Bay, I didn't dare glance at TJ to see how *he* was doing in the blush department. I just took the fact that he was saying nothing to mean that his brain was so weighed down with sheer mortification that it was squeezing any other thoughts right out of his head.

I mean, yes, so the you-know-what might have got us out of a whole lot of trouble, but that didn't mean either of us could handle it happening. Especially *me*; I couldn't believe I'd actually told a boy to *ki*—

But before I relived the sheer, shameful shame of it all again, there was that first, menacing swoop.

"Oh, God!" TJ groaned, crouching lower to the ground. "Not that stupid bird again!"

"Just be glad he didn't come after you when the police were around. We'd *definitely* have been spotted then!" I said, bending warily too, though I didn't really think the seagull was remotely interested in me. "Hey, look – isn't this your street?"

Great. In a few seconds, TJ would be safely away from flapping wings and pointy beaks, and I would be safely away from him, and could get on with pretending that the you-know-what had never happened. (Ha! Like it would be *that* easy. . .)

"Er, I'm not really up for going home right now," said TJ, pushing his floppy hair off his face and gazing in the direction of his flat. "I just managed to avoid getting grilled by the police. I don't really want a grilling from my mum about where I've been. . ."

Having met TJ's mum again at the flat a little while ago, I kind of understood what he meant. We'd both been shaken up by what had happened (watching Sam and his gang getting arrested, I mean, not the you-know-what), and the thought of Mrs O'Connell twittering and scolding was exhausting just to *think* about, never mind hear.

"Well . . . you could come back to mine for a bit, if you want!"

I felt like I *had* to suggest that . . . you-know-what or *no* you-know-what, me and TJ'd been through so much together in the last little while that I couldn't just leave him on his own, aimlessly wandering the town.

And so nine dive-bombing attempts and a steep, winding road later and we were nearly at my house.

"He *hates* me," moaned TJ, straightening up after dive-bomb number ten. "How long do those things live for? It's going to follow me around till *one* of us dies!"

"Hey, you chucked a stone at it, remember? No *wonder* it hates you!"

We were just about level with the little alleyway that ran at the back of my garden, I was vaguely aware.

"It was an *accident*!" said TJ, raising his shoulders in a show of innocence. "I'm not a rock-chucking kind of person, if you hadn't noticed!"

I'd noticed all right. Actually, *everyone* who'd passed us on the way here had noticed that, even if they didn't understand what they were seeing. Both knees of his jeans being green was a bit of a clue. *That's* what you get when you're crawling away from trouble at high speed through a garden. By comparison, my bare knees were pink – not 'cause of blushing, but because I scrubbed the grass stains off them in the sea with a handful of sand after the coast was clear and the police and Sam's gang had gone. Whatever; green and pink knees were a proud badge of innocence as far as me and TJ were concerned.

"OK, OK, so it wasn't deliberate. So you've got to show the gull you're sorry. Get him to be your friend!" I said, relaxing now that we both seemed to be ignoring the you-know-what.

"And how do I do that?" asked TJ, completely perplexed.

The faintest sugary scent of peaches 'n' cream put the idea in my head.

"Sweet-talk him," I told TJ, catching sight of a bundle of ginger fur on a wall down the alley.

"Sweet-talk him? What's *that* supposed to mean?"

Confusion brought TJ and his baseball boots grinding to a halt on the crunchy gravel.

"For a start, look up at him," I said, stopping too.

With a guarded glare at me, TJ did what he was told and stared up.

"Urgh . . . he's staring back at me."

"No – that's *good*. Now you've got to smile."

Poor TJ; he was so desperate for the gull to get over the grudge that he seemed to be willing to do anything (stupid) that I told him to do.

"Stella . . . I'm smiling, but I think it's just making him angry!" said TJ through a wide, forced, teeth-gritted grin.

"Hold on. . ." I said, rummaging in my rucksack for the magic ingredient that I thought would make all the difference.

"Stella! He's coming straight down! He's going to dive-bomb me again!"

Sure enough, the gull had tucked in his wings and was hurtling down at high speed in our – OK, just *TJ*'s – direction.

"Here! Hold this straight out!" I ordered him, shoving a mini fairy cake in his hand.

I don't know if birds have brakes, but the seagull seemed to put *his* on. One glimpse of the outstretched fairy cake and he swooped *out* of his death-defying beak-first dive and tilted backwards into an elegant flap of wings, hovering just close enough to TJ's hand to gently grab the cake from between his quivering fingers.

"Prrrp!" prrrped Peaches approvingly, ambling along the wall – of the house opposite ours – to get a better look at what was going on.

"What just happened?" TJ asked warily, as the seagull settled itself on the top of the nearest street-lamp to gulp its snack down.

"I think you just made a friend. . ." I grinned at TJ, hoping he understood that I didn't just mean the bird. "And if you ever fancy joining the circus, you've got a great act – 'TJ and his Amazing, Guzzling Gull!'"

Thud-a-thud-a-THUD-a-THUD-a-THUD . . . *TWANGGGGG! DOOF.*

I looked at TJ; TJ looked at me. Peaches looked slant-eyed down at *both* of us, as if he was daring us to finally find out what all the noises were about in the sumo-wrestling poltergeists' holiday home.

"Look – down the alleyway! The door in the wall is open! We could sneak into the garden and check it out!"

I *meant* to say, "Absolutely no *way* – do you want us to get arrested for trespassing and end up in the cell next door to Sam's lot?", but instead I said, "OK." (After what had gone on at Sugar Bay I think I must still have had excess adrenaline shooting around in my system. Well, that's the only excuse *I* can think of.)

So me and TJ were back to crouching – if not quite crawling – through shrubbery for the second time today.

Thud-a-thud-a-THUD-a-THUD-a-THUD . . . TWANGGGGG! DOOF.

"It's coming from that room!" I hissed to TJ, as I pointed to the ground-floor window with the curtains drawn shut – the same one he'd tried to peek in from the wall this morning, before we fell out over my mobile.

Above us on the wall, Peaches mimicked our tiptoeing, stealthily padding his fat, furry way along the top of the brickwork.

"If we get up close, we'll probably be able to see through the gap in the curtains," TJ turned and whispered to me.

Slowly, slowly, hearts pounding somewhere in our throats, me and TJ lifted our heads above the windowsill and. . .

"EEEEEEEKKKKK!"

That was me, getting the fright of my thirteen-year-old life as a sweet-toothed seagull landed on my backpack with a thunk, and started pecking at the buckle to release the other fairy cakes it somehow knew were in there.

"AAAAAAARGHHHH!"

That was TJ, as the curtains were pulled open and a *terrifying* face glared out at us. . .

CHAPTER 21

And for my next trick. . . (Oof!)

Omigod. We were in the lair of the sumo-wrestling poltergeists.

Rumble-rumble-rumble-rumble-rumble-rumble-THUNK!

"Want a try?"

Er, to be honest, close up, the friendly, sporty-looking woman holding the unicycle out to TJ didn't look much like a sumo-wrestler *or* a poltergeist.

"Er, OK, Mrs Mystic . . . er, Mrs Marzipan. . ." said TJ warily, sneaking a quick worried glance at me before he clambered up on the one-wheeled bike she was holding steady for him.

"I told you, just call me Bev," said Bev, now giving him a gentle push off.

TJ only made it to *rumble-THUNK!* No – he didn't even make it to *THUNK!*, 'cause *THUNK!* had been the noise Mrs Mystic Marzipan (Bev) had made when she hopped elegantly off the unicycle as she demonstrated it to us just now. With TJ, it was more of a *rumble-"Oooof! Owwww . . ."*.

"What about you, Stella? Fancy a go on the trampette?" asked Mr Mystic Marzipan (otherwise known as John, otherwise known as the person with the terrifying face). "Maybe you could try a double somersault! You look like you're pretty agile, the way you scramble out of your bedroom window all the time, like that cat of yours!"

Urgh . . . so I thought *I* was the one doing the spying on *them*, but the people in this house had done a much better job of spotting what everyone in *our* house was up to. And speaking of that cat of mine, it turned out that Peaches was already on purring terms with the Marzipans – he'd been in and out all week, they said. He was sitting at their open window now, catching a few rays on his ginger fur while he idly watched TJ make a fool of himself.

"Um, I don't think so," I said, shaking my head shyly, as I stared at the trampette and the banner behind it that read "*Meet the Marvellous, Magical, Mystic Marzipans!!!*"

"Well, I don't think we'll be asking these two to join our act, darling!" Bev joked with her husband, while smiling down at TJ, who was trying to disentangle himself from the unicycle.

"No, I don't think so," said Mr Mystic Marzipan, his smile scarily wide. "And they're a bit too noisy to make good private detectives!"

Nabbed by clowns – can you believe it?

It was the seagull's fault of course, and no faked kisses could get me and TJ out of trouble when the window flew open and Mr Mystic Marzipan and his white clown face loomed out at us.

"What's this?" he'd boomed cheerfully. "Trying to get a sneak preview of the show or something? Better come in then!"

We'd looked at each other, then at the loud and gaudy props and Punch & Judy stall inside.

"Tell you what," Bev had said, appearing at the window. "You live across the lane with your family, don't you? Why don't you pop across and invite your parents and those cute little boys over?"

And that's what we did. And that's why Dad was practising juggling in the corner just now, while Mum was attempting to stop Jake and Jamie from clobbering each other with the Punch & Judy puppets. And that's how we'd come to find out that Mr and Mrs Mystic Marzipan had been rehearsing their circus skills in the house they'd rented on the other side of the back lane. They'd been booked to appear in all sorts of shows and events during the Portbay Gala in a week or two's time, and had been just in the middle of perfecting their latest balancing act when me and TJ and a very greedy seagull had nearly put a sudden end to their careers.

"Think my entire *bum* might be bruised. . ." said TJ, finally untangling himself from the unicycle with a bit of help from Bev.

"Probably serves you right!" grinned Dad, still keeping his eyes fixed to the clubs he was juggling. "It's kind of dangerous to give people surprises, specially when their wife's trying to do a backflip on to their shoulders!"

Dad was right of course, but how were we meant to have known? It's not *every* day you find yourself with a backflipping, fire-eating acrobatic clown act living in the house at the bottom of the garden.

"Ah, now don't be too hard on them," said Mr Mystic Marzipan, giving me and TJ a wink as he took off his red nose and gave his real nose a scratch. "I'm sure we all got up to some mischief or other when we were young!"

And then it hit me – it was *exactly* the right time to ask Dad the question.

"Dad . . . what happened with you and the paintballing thing? When you were fifteen?"

There was a deafening clatter as the clubs fell out of sync, out of Dad's hands and on to the floor.

Dad looked horrified. Mum looked like she might burst out laughing. Mr and Mrs Mystic Marzipan and TJ looked confused. Jake and Jamie carried on hitting each other with puppets.

"Before you ask, Andy, *I* didn't tell Stella!" said Mum, as she wrestled Punch off Jake's hand.

(Jamie had just spotted Peaches and was running over to him, brandishing Judy. With an elegant "floop!", Peaches did an impressive disappearing trick that the Mystic Marzipans would be proud of.)

"Auntie V said I should ask you," I told Dad, solving the mystery for him.

I held my breath, waiting for him to speak. Back in London, Dad was a smart, sussed, suited lawyer who never got flummoxed, but right here right now I'd never seen him look so sheepish. (Well, apart from when he sledgehammered through a pipe and flooded the house last week, or when he used his head to dismantle the toilet, of course.)

"I . . ." he began, rolling his eyes upwards so he was talking to the ceiling. "I . . . I mean, me and my friends at the time . . . we thought it would be a laugh to go out with these paintballing guns and . . . and splat a flock of sheep."

"*Sheep*?" The word came out of TJ's mouth with a squeak and a giggle (a squiggle?).

"And before you ask, Stella, none of them were hurt – your dad and his friends weren't close enough to do any real damage, thankfully," Mum explained, while Dad shuffled and blushed.

"They were just a bit scared. And multi-coloured, by the time we'd finished," Dad mumbled, acting as shamefaced and shifty as a schoolkid who's been caught writing rude words on the loo door. "The farmer went mad at us – never mind your gran and grandad. . ."

As sorry as I felt for those poor, bemused sheep, I couldn't stop the giggle that was vibrating its way up my chest. Not that anyone could hear it, not above the booming laughs of Mr Mystic Marzipan and his missus, which of course got everyone else started (no surprise, since it's in clowns' job descriptions to laugh a lot, isn't it?).

Anyway, Auntie V was right – it *had* been worth waiting for. I'd never be able to take my dad seriously again, and I think he pretty much knew it.

"Wait till I get hold of that sister of mine. . ." said Dad suddenly, laughing too, his cheeks still telltale pink. "Your Auntie V's got a lot to answer for!"

TJ was leaning on the bucking unicycle and grinning, without having a clue who we were on about. Course, how could he know that without Auntie V – and all her advice – me and him might not be friends? I mean, thanks to her, I was Stella, and TJ was my etc.

But you know something?

If TJ *was* going to be my friend, there was one thing he was going to have to do for sure; same as me.

He'd *better* keep pretending that emergency kiss *never* happened. . .

From: Frankie
To: *stella*
Subject: The great mobile mystery SOLVED!!

Hi Stella!

So it was just TJ I was talking to? Boo . . . there I was thinking it was some secret boyfriend you hadn't told me about, and all the time it was Portbay's biggest teen gangsta (OK, make that teen *hamster*).

Still can't believe TJ had the cheek to nick your mobile off you though. If I'd known I was speaking to a thief I'd have said more than "Hi, is Stella there?" before he hung up on me! But I guess after reading all that stuff in the attachment, I kind of think I might *possibly* reckon TJ's all right now . . . sorry, but I can't help being protective!

Better go – Mum's due back soon and I promised to take a turn cleaning Peetie's cage out. I haven't started yet, but you know how it is – cleaning out parakeet poop or watching MTV with a packet of Munchies . . . not much contest, is there?

Miss you ☹, but M8s 4eva ☺!
Frankie

PS Tell Peaches I found one of his hairs in my toothbrush the other night(?!).

PPS Parminder says she phoned you yesterday, and you told her that some girl called Rachel and her mates are giving you hassle. Want me to come down and sort them out? You know me – wouldn't let anyone take the mick out of you. Why isn't TJ standing up for you? Oh, that's right – you said he's kind of on the short side. Couldn't he just go and bite their ankles, then? Ha!